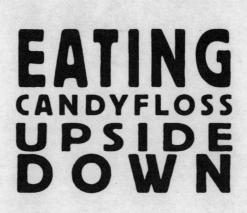

EATING
CANDYFLOSS
UPSIDE
DOWN

A Carousel of Stories and Poems

D0279917

PUFFIN BOOKS

Published by the Penguin Group
Penguin Books Ltd, 80 Strand, London WC2R 0RL, England
Penguin Putnam Inc., 375 Hudson Street, New York, New York 10014, USA
Penguin Books Australia Ltd, 250 Camberwell Road, Camberwell, Victoria 3124, Australia
Penguin Books Canada Ltd, 10 Alcorn Avenue, Toronto, Ontario, Canada M4V 3B2
Penguin Books India (P) Ltd, 11 Community Centre, Panchsheel Park,
New Delhi – 110 017, India
Penguin Books (NZ) Ltd, Cnr Rosedale and Airborne Roads, Albany, Auckland, New Zealand
Penguin Books (South Africa) (Pty) Ltd, 24 Sturdee Avenue, Rosebank 2196, South Africa

Penguin Books Ltd, Registered Offices: 80 Strand, London WC2R 0RL, England

www.penguin.com

First published 2003
1

Set in Usherwood Book

Made and printed in England by Clays Ltd, St Ives plc

British Library Cataloguing in Publication Data
A CIP catalogue record for this book is available from the British Library

ISBN 0-141-31478-8

EATING
CANDYFLOSS
UPSIDE
DOWN

A Carousel of Stories and Poems

Edited by *Carousel* Magazine

PUFFIN BOOKS

For details of subscribing to *Carousel*
please telephone 0121 622 7458
or e-mail carousel.guide@virgin.net.

Carousel Editorial Team: Jenny and David Blanch,
Val Bierman, Enid Stephenson, Pat Thomson and
Chris Stephenson.

introduction

This collection of stories, poems and illustrations celebrates the twenty-fifth issue of *Carousel: The Guide to Children's Books*. Carousel is produced in full colour three times a year and offers a guide to the best books around and an insight into authors' and illustrators' work.

Since 1995 interviews and features have appeared in the magazine reflecting the immense range of children's books. We asked some of those who had been featured if they would provide a story, poem or illustration and, without exception, they immediately agreed. So this collection celebrates the wealth of talent and generosity in the children's book world, as well as providing a brilliant introduction, if introduction is needed, to many of our best writers and illustrators.

All monies raised will go to the Birmingham Children's Hospital, which has child patients from all over the country and is a pioneer in many key fields of medicine.

Enjoy and keep on reading!

contents

contents

THE ODD ONE OUT

by Jacqueline Wilson
illustrated by Nick Sharratt

I'm the odd one out in the family. There are a lot of us. OK, here goes. There's my mum and my stepdad Graham and my big brother Mark and my big sister Ginnie and my little sister Jess and my big stepbrother Jon and my big stepsister Alice and then there's my little half-sister Cherry and my baby half-brother Rupert. Not to mention my real dad's new baby and his girlfriend Gina's twins, but they live in Cornwall now so I only see them for holidays. *Long* holidays, like summer and sometimes Christmas and Easter. Not short bank holidays, like today. It's a bank holiday and that means an Outing.

I hate Outings. I like *Innings*. My idea of bliss would be to read my book in bed with a packet of Pop Tarts for breakfast, get up late and draw or colour or write stories, have bacon sandwiches and crisps and a big cream cake or two for lunch, read all afternoon, have a whole chocolate Swiss roll for tea in front of the telly, draw or colour or write more stories, and then pizza for supper.

I've never enjoyed a day like that. It wouldn't work,

anyway, because there are far too many of us if we all stay indoors and the big ones hog the sofa and the comfy chairs and the little ones are always dashing around and yelling and grabbing my felt tips. And Mum is always trying to stop me eating all the food I like best, pretending that a plate of lettuce and carrots and celery is just as yummy as pizza (!) and Graham is always suggesting I might like to get on this bike he bought me and go for a ride.

I wish he'd get on *his* bike. And take the whole family with him. And most of mine. Imagine if it was just Mum and me . . .

We had to do a piece of autobiographical writing at school last week on *My Family*. I pondered for a bit. Just writing down the *names* of my family would take up half the page. I wanted to write a proper story, not an autobiographical list. So I had an imaginary cull of my entire family apart from Mum and wrote about our life together as a teeny-weeny two-people family. I went into painstaking detail, writing about birthdays and Christmas and how my mum sometimes produced presents that had *Love from Daddy* or *Best wishes from Auntie Kylie in Australia* – although I knew she'd really bought them herself. I even pretended that Mum sometimes played at being my Gran or even Grandpa and I played at being her son or her little baby. I wrote that although we played these games it was just for fun. We weren't lonely at all. We positively *loved* being such a small family.

Mrs Mann positively loved my effort too! This was a

surprise because Mrs Mann is very, very strict. She's the oldest teacher at school and she can be really scary and sarcastic. You can't mess around in Mrs Mann's class. She wears these neat grey suits that match her grey hair and white blouses with tidily tied bows and a pearl brooch precisely centred on her lapel. You can tell just by looking at her that she's a stickler for punctuation and spelling and paragraphing and all those other boring, boring, boring things that stop you getting on with the story. My *Family* piece had its fair share of mistakes ringed in Mrs Mann's red rollerball but she *still* gave me ten out of ten because she said it was such a vivid truthful piece of heartfelt autobiographical writing.

I felt a little fidgety about this. Vivid it might be, but truthful it *isn't*. When Mrs Mann was talking about my small family, my friends Amy and Kate stared at me open-mouthed because I'm always whining on to them about my *big* family. Luckily, they're not telltales.

I can't stick telltales. My little sister, Jess, is the worst ever. She's always rushing to Mum whimpering that I won't share my chocolate with her or that I poked her with my pencil or hit her on the head with my book because she kept on and on pestering me. I can't stick my big sister, Ginnie, either, because she's always sneering at me and trying to squash me – though when we have a fight I often manage to sit on top of her and then I squash *her*. I'm not just sisterist. I can't stick my brother, Mark, either.

Sometimes I get on better with all my Steps. My big stepbrother, Jon, likes Art too and he always says sweet things about my drawings. My big stepsister, Alice, isn't bad either. One day when we were all bored she did my hair in these cool little plaits with beads and ribbons and made up my face so I looked almost grown up. Yes, I like Jon and Alice, but they're much older than me so they don't really want me hanging out with them.

The Halfies aren't bad either. I quite like sitting Cherry on my lap and reading her *Where the Wild Things Are*. She always squeals when I roar their terrible roars right in her ear and Mum gets cross but Cherry *likes* it. Rupert isn't into books yet – in fact I was a bit miffed when I showed him my old nursery-rhyme book and he *bit* it, like he thought it was a big bright sandwich. He's not really fun to play with yet because he's too little.

That's the trouble. Mark and Ginnie and Jon and Alice are too big. Jess and Cherry and Rupert are too little. I'm the Piggy in the Middle.

Hmm. My unpleasant brother, Mark, frequently makes grunting snorty noises at me and calls me Fatty Pigling.

I have highly inventive nicknames for Mark, indeed, for *all* my family (apart from Mum) but I'd better not write them down or you'll be shocked.

I said a few very rude words to myself when Mum and Graham said we were going for a l-o-n-g walk along the river for our bank holiday outing. It's OK for Rupert. He goes in the buggy. It's OK for Cherry and Jess. They get piggyback rides the minute they start whining. It's OK for Mark and Ginnie and Jon and Alice. They stride ahead in a little gang (or lag behind, whatever) and they talk about music and football and s-e-x and whenever I edge up to them they say, 'Push off, Pigling,' if they're Mark or Ginnie, or, 'Hi, Laura, off you go now,' if they're Jon or Alice.

I'd love it if it could just be Mum and me going on a walk together. But Graham is always around and he makes silly jokes or slaps me on the back or bosses me about. Sometimes I get really narked and tell him he's not my dad so he can't tell me what to do. Other times I just *look* at him. Looks can be very effective.

My face was contorted in a *dark scowl* all the long, long, long trudge along the river. It was so incredibly boring. I am past the age of going 'duck duck duck' whenever a bird with wings flies past. I am not yet of the age to collapse into giggles when some dark-shaded male language students say hello in sexy foreign accents (Ginnie and Alice) and I don't stare gape-mouthed when a pretty girl in a bikini waves from a boat (Mark and Jon).

I just stomped along wearily, surreptitiously eating a Galaxy . . . and then a Kit Kat . . . and a couple of Rolos. I handed the rest round to the family like a good generous girl. That's another huge disadvantage of large families. Offer your packet of Rolos round once and they're nearly all gone in one fell swoop.

We went to this pub garden for lunch and I golloped down a couple of cheese toasties and two packets of crisps and two Cokes – all this fresh air had made me peckish – and I had to stoke myself up for the long trail back home along the river.

'Oh, we thought we'd go via the Green Fields,' said Graham.

I groaned.

'Graham! It's *miles*! And I've got serious blisters already.'

'I think you might like the Green Fields this particular Monday,' said Mum.

She and Graham smiled.

I didn't smile back. I *don't* like the Green Fields. They are just what their name implies. Two big green fields joined by a line of poplar trees. They don't even have a playground with swings. There isn't even an ice cream van. There's just a lot of *grass*.

But guess what, guess what! When we got nearer the Green Fields I heard this buzz and clatter and music and laughter. And *then* I smelt wonderful mouth-watering fried onions. We turned the corner – and the Green Fields were so full you couldn't see a glimpse of grass! There was a fair there for the bank holiday.

I gave a whoop. Mark and Ginnie and Jon and Alice gave a whoop too, though they were half mocking me. Jess and Cherry gave great big whoops. Baby Rupert whooped too. He couldn't see the fair down at kneecap level in his buggy, but he didn't want to be left out.

Mum and Graham smiled smugly.

Of course the fair meant different things to all of us. Jon and Mark – *and* Graham – wanted to go straight on the dodgems. Ginnie and Alice and I went too, while Mum minded the littlies. She bought them all whippy ice creams with chocolate flakes. I wailed, saying I'd much, much, much sooner have an ice cream than get in a dodgem car. Mum sighed and bought me an ice cream too. But as soon as it was in my hand I decided it *might* be fun to go on the dodgems too, so I jumped in beside Jon.

Big mistake. Mark drove straight into us, wham bam, and then splat, the chocolate flake went right up my nostril and my ice cream went all over my face.

Mum mopped me up with one of Rupert's wet wipes, and Jon bought me another ice cream to console me. I licked this in peace while Jess and Cherry and baby Rupert sat on a kiddies' roundabout and slowly and solemnly revolved in giant teacups.

'I wonder if they've got a *proper* roundabout,' said Mum. 'I used to love those ones with the horses and the twisty gilt rails and the special music. I want to go on a real old-fashioned carousel.'

'Oh, Mum, you don't get those any more,' said Ginnie – but she was *wrong*.

We went on all sorts of *new*-fashioned rides first. We were all hurtled round and round and upside down until even I started wondering if that extra ice cream had been such a good idea. Then, as we staggered queasily to the other side of the field, we heard old organ music. Mum lifted her head, listening intently.

'Is it?' she said.

It *was*. We pushed through the crowd and suddenly it was just like stepping back a hundred years. There was the most beautiful old roundabout with galloping horses with grinning mouths and flaring nostrils and scarlet saddles, some shiny black, some chocolate brown, some dappled grey. There was also one odd pink ostrich with crimson feathers and an orange beak.

'Why is that big bird there, Mum?' I asked.

'I don't know, Laura. I think they always have one odd one. Maybe it's a tradition.'

'I'm going to go on the bird,' I said.

The roundabout was slowing down. Mum had little Rupert unbuckled from his buggy so he could ride too. Graham had Cherry in his arms. Mark and Jon said the roundabout was just for kids, but when Graham asked one of them to look after Jess they both offered eagerly. Ginnie and Alice had an argument over who was going to ride on a black horse with Robbie on his nameplate (they both have a thing about Robbie Williams) so eventually they squeezed on together.

I rushed for the ostrich. I didn't need to. No one else wanted it. Well, *I* did. I clambered on and stroked its crimson feathers. Ostriches are definitely the odd ones out of the bird family. They can't fly. They're too heavy for their own wings.

I'm definitely the odd one out of my family – and I frequently feel too heavy for my own legs. I sat gripping the ostrich with my knees, waiting for the music to start and the roundabout to start revolving. People were still scrabbling on to the few remaining horses. A middle-aged lady in much-too-tight jeans was hauling this little toddler up on to the platform. I put out my hand to help – and then stopped, astonished. I couldn't have been more amazed if my ostrich had opened its beak and

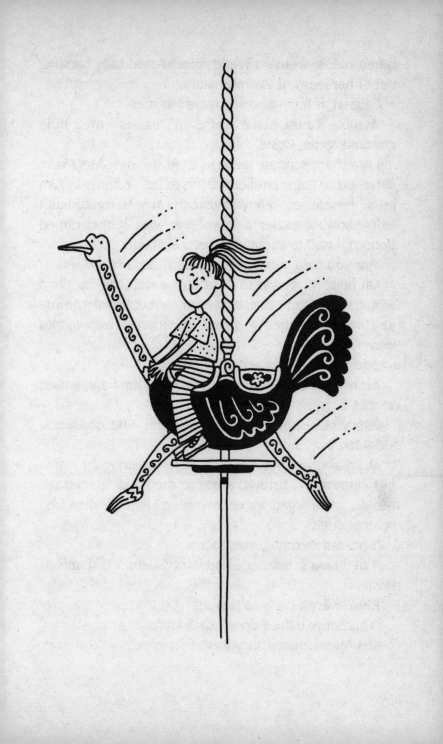

bitten me. It wasn't any old middle-aged lady bursting out of her jeans. It was Mrs Mann!

I stared at her – and she stared at me.

'Hello, Laura,' she said. 'This is my little granddaughter, Rosie.'

I made appropriate remarks to Rosie while Mrs Mann struggled to get them both up on to the ordinary brown horse beside my splendid ostrich. Mrs Mann couldn't help showing rather a lot of her vast blue-denimed bottom. I had to struggle to keep a straight face.

'Are you with your mother, Laura?' said Mrs Mann.

Oh help! Mum was in front of me with Rupert. I had written Mrs Mann that long essay about Mum and me just living together. I hadn't mentioned any babies whatsoever.

'I'm here . . . on my own,' I mumbled.

At that exact moment Mum turned round and waved at me.

'Are you all right, Laura?' she called. She nodded at Mrs Mann.

Mum and Mrs Mann looked at me, waiting for me to introduce them. I stayed silent as the music started up. *Go, go, go*, I urged inside my head. But we didn't go soon enough.

'I'm Laura's mum,' said Mum.

'I'm Laura's teacher,' said Mrs Mann. 'And this is Rosie.'

Rosie waved coyly to Rupert.

'This is my baby, Rupert,' said Mum.

Mrs Mann looked surprised.

'And that's Cherry over there with my partner Graham and Jess with my son Mark and that's my stepson Jon and then that's Alice and Ginnie over there, waving at those boys, the naughty girls. Sorry! We're such a big family now that it's a bit hard for anyone to take in,' said Mum, because Mrs Mann was looking so stunned.

The horses started to edge forward very, very slowly, u-u-u-u-p and d-o-w-n. My tummy went up and down too as Mrs Mann looked at me.

'So you're part of a very big family, Laura?' she said.

'Yes, Mrs Mann,' I said, in a very small voice.

'Well, you *do* surprise me,' she said.

'Nana, Nana!' said Rosie, taking hold of Mrs Mann's nose and wiggling it backwards and forwards affectionately. Mrs Mann simply chuckled. I wondered how she'd react if any of our class tweaked her nose!

'We seem to be surprising each other,' shouted Mrs Mann, while the music got louder as the roundabout revved up. 'Well, Laura, judging by your long and utterly convincing autobiographical essay, you are obviously either a pathological liar – or a born writer. We'll give you the benefit of the doubt. You have the most vivid imagination of any child I've ever taught. You will obviously go far.'

And then the music was too loud for talking and the horses whirled round and round and round. I sat tight on my ostrich and it spread its crimson wings and we flew far over the fair, all the way up and over the moon.

MERRY-GO-ROUND

by **Dick King-Smith**
illustrated by **Helen Oxenbury**

When I was round about three or four,
I went to a fairground and there I saw
A roundabout spinning around like a top,
And I said to my dad, 'Make it stop! Make it stop!
I want to get on!' And my dad said, 'Of course.'
And it stopped and I got on a pink and green
    horse
And around and around I went galloping fast
And I waved to my dad every time I went past,
And I shouted and shouted and shouted with
    joy –
There was never so happy a roundabout boy.
I'd never been quite so excited before,
When I was round about three or four.

THE GHOST TRAIN

by **Eva Ibbotson**
illustrated by **Mairi Hedderwick**

It was an old-fashioned fair, the kind that travels from town to town, but it had everything that children needed. It had roundabouts with dappled horses, a tower that you could slide down on a coconut mat and shooting booths where you could win huge fluffy rabbits or some goldfish in a bowl.

And, of course, it had a ghost train.

When it was new it was a very good ghost train. It had skulls with eye sockets that lit up, skeletons that touched the children with ghastly fingers and a machine which made an unspeakable howling noise, like people being tortured in a very nasty way, just before the carriages came out again into the light.

The ghost train belonged to a man called Albert Fisher, who ran it with his ten-year-old son, Felix. There had been ghost trains in the Fisher family as far back as anyone could remember, and Mr Fisher meant to hand the business on to Felix as soon as he was old enough.

But the world was changing. The children who came

to ride on the ghost train now were not so easily scared and when they came out again they told their parents that it had been a waste of time, and that put off other children. There were days now when only three or four children paid to go into the tunnel and sometimes there were none at all.

So Mr Fisher made less and less money. And the less money he made, the shabbier the skeletons became so that their fingers began to drop off, and the eye sockets of the skulls didn't light up properly, and the machine which made a ghastly howling noise went on the blink and couldn't be mended.

Even so, the Fishers might have managed – but a new attraction had arrived at the fair. It was twice as big as anything else in the fairground, and twice as noisy, and it was called the Tunnel of Hate.

The Tunnel of Hate had everything terrifying that you could think of. It had carcasses hanging from hooks and gaping mouths dribbling blood and piercing green lights that blinded the children as they went in. There were machines which made thumps and screams and groans so loud that the tunnel shook with them and quite often the children came out so shaken and giddy and deafened that they were sick.

The man who owned it was called Nobby Fell. He had a red face and a fat mouth and there was nothing he wouldn't do for money. He'd been in prison twice and he didn't care how sick the children were when they came out of his tunnel, as long as they paid.

'Call that a ghost train?' Nobby Fell would sneer,

swaggering past Mr Fisher and his son. 'Looks more like a caterpillar with the chickenpox. Why don't you give it a lick of paint?'

But Mr Fisher didn't have the money for a lick of paint. He didn't have the money for anything – and the day came when Mr Fisher told his son that they couldn't go on.

'Soon we won't be able to buy the petrol to get us to the next place,' he said. 'We'll have to sell up for what we can get and maybe I could get a job in a factory or something.'

But he was very sad. Travelling with a fair is something that gets into your blood and he had so wanted to pass the ghost train on to Felix.

Felix agreed with his father; he knew that things were desperate. But he said, 'Do you think we could manage to stay with the fair till we get to Dunsterhaven next week? I've got a sort of an idea.'

So his father said, all right, just one more time, and at the end of the week they packed the ghost train on to the lorries and followed on in their caravan till they reached Dunsterhaven.

It was a small grey town on the border between Scotland and England, and on a hill to the north of it was an outcrop of steep rocks known as Dunster Crags. Not many people went up there; it was a place where there had been fighting between the English and the Scots in the olden days. Now all that was left was a tumbledown house lived in by a single family known as the MacDuffs.

.... all that was left was
a tumble-down house....

Felix had met them when he went exploring two years ago and had made friends with them. Mostly, the MacDuffs kept themselves to themselves, but they liked Felix, who was not nosy or interfering, and now whenever the fair came to the town he climbed up to the crag and paid them a visit.

'Come in, boy, come in,' said MacDuff, who was the head of the family. He was a huge man with a very whiskery beard and very hairy legs, which sprouted out below his kilt, and he was carrying an axe because he had been chopping firewood.

Felix followed him into the house and the rest of the family gathered round to welcome him. There was Granny MacDuff who was so old that she was bald and had only a single tooth, which was screwed into her lower jaw and often got lost, causing her a lot of trouble.

There was MacDuff's little daughter, Polly, a tomboy who was always turning somersaults or climbing on the furniture – and MacDuff's uncle who was in a wheelchair and had some disease which made his head wobble, but he was a nice man all the same.

And there was the family dog, Satan: a huge black mastiff with slobbering jowls and a tongue that seemed to go on and on . . .

Felix thought it was best to come straight to the point and when he had asked how they all were, and they had said they were as well as could be expected, he said, 'I want to ask you a favour. It's a big one, I'm afraid.'

MacDuff put down his axe and Granny MacDuff picked up her ear trumpet.

But when Felix had told them what he wanted, they all shook their heads.

'I don't think we could do that,' said MacDuff.

'It's not what we've been used to,' said Granny MacDuff.

'No, it's not what we've been used to at all,' said the uncle with the very wobbly head.

Felix waited.

Then, 'It would mean so much to my father and me,' he said. 'We're really desperate. And maybe you'd enjoy it. I mean, it would be a change.'

The family looked at each other and sighed. Then Polly, who had been standing on her head, said, 'I wouldn't mind doing it. It could be interesting.'

'Well, you're certainly not doing it without us,' said her father.

And after some more discussion, the MacDuffs agreed to do what Felix had asked of them.

Mr Fisher couldn't understand it. They'd been at Dunsterhaven for five days and each day they took more money.

'It's nice in there,' a little girl said as she came out. 'The people are spooky and scary like real ghosts and they do splendid tricks.'

'I like the man in the wheelchair who takes off his head,' said her sister. 'The way he puts it on his knee and pats it; it's really cool, that.'

'No, the dog's best,' said a boy sitting in the carriage behind them. 'When he comes along with his tongue lolling and his eyes flashing and pretends to take bites out of you, he's terrifying.'

And they went and told their friends and the children in their school, and every day more and more people came to ride on Mr Fisher's ghost train. One boy went round six times because he thought the dog who was pretending to be a ghost dog was so clever and well trained.

'Really, it's awfully good of your friends to help us out like that, especially when I can pay so little,' said Mr Fisher. 'You'd think they'd been pretending to be ghosts for years. I suppose they must have been trained in conjuring and magic?'

'Not really,' said Felix. 'They're just a very intelligent family.'

But of course Nobby Fell, who owned the Tunnel of

Hate, was getting angrier and angrier. Every day more people went on the ghost train and fewer and fewer went into the Tunnel of Hate. The truth was that in the Tunnel of Hate everything was always exactly the same: the same carcasses, the same mouths dribbling blood, the same hoots and whistles . . . whereas in the ghost train you never knew what you were going to get. Sometimes it would be a bald old lady trying to find her tooth and gibbering while she hunted, or it might be the little girl hanging upside down from the ceiling and making the lights go out . . . or a hairy man in a kilt swiping his axe down on people's heads.

And quite soon Nobby got so angry that he decided to do something. 'It's a swindle,' he said to the men who worked for him. 'It's a complete swindle, those people in there doing tricks and pretending to be ghosts. I'm going to put an end to it.'

'How are you going to do that, gov'nor?' said one of the men.

'Never you mind,' said Nobby. 'I've got my methods.'

Nobby's methods were not pleasant. He was a petty crook on the side, and he kept a loaded gun in his caravan.

Now he hid it in his coat pocket and waited till the ghost train was shutting up for the night. Then he went over to Mr Fisher with an oily smile and asked if he could go round once by himself because he'd heard such good things about what went on inside.

'I'll buy a ticket, of course,' he said. 'I wouldn't expect to go round for free.'

Felix would have smelled a rat, but Felix had gone into the town and Mr Fisher, who was too trusting for his own good, said yes he could go round once before everyone went home.

Nobby got into the first carriage. The ghost train swooped into the darkness – and a terrible old woman with no hair appeared in front of Nobby. She was the ugliest, baldest old woman he had ever seen and now she thrust her face in front of Nobby and opened her mouth.

'Tooth!' she screamed. 'Tooth, tooth; they've stolen my tooth!'

And Nobby let off his gun. He did not fire directly at the old woman; he knew that he couldn't go murdering people who worked in a ghost train without being caught, but he thought if he frightened them enough, they would run away in terror and never come back. And indeed the old woman did give a horrible screech and disappeared into the darkness, but instead of her there came a man in a wheelchair who began playing around with his head. He unscrewed it from his neck; he threw it up in the air, he caught it and screwed it on again . . .

This made Nobby so angry that he let off two bursts from his gun. Pretending to take off your head is trickery of the worst sort. It is cheating. When he fired his gun this time the bullet only just missed the side of the invalid chair, and the old man wheeled himself away, using some rather nasty language.

But it was the man in the kilt who did it for Nobby.

A great hairy man with an axe which he raised higher and higher, ready to bring it down on Nobby's head . . .

And Nobby lost his nerve. He didn't fire above the man's head or to the side of him – he fired directly at his chest.

The bullet went in just above the heart. There was an unearthly scream, a flash of light, fountains of blood – and then the man dropped his axe and fell like a stone to the floor.

'Oh Lord,' said Nobby. He had aimed and hit and killed – and now the police would get him.

Only they wouldn't. He'd been alone in the tunnel. No one could prove it was him – not if he could get away at once.

He jumped out of the carriage and crawled along the side of the tunnel, sweating with fear. Now he could see a glimmer of light in the entrance; he was nearly there – he was out . . .

Nobby straightened himself and, as he did so, something incredible happened. The man he had shot and killed a few minutes before rose up before him. He had his axe in his hand and his face was livid with rage.

'How dare you,' he thundered. 'How dare you shoot at the MacDuffs of Dunster, you cowardly imbecile! Say your prayers because your hour has come!'

And he flexed his arm, ready to raise his axe.

Nobby gasped. Spittle came from his mouth. 'You

can't . . . be . . . there,' he squealed. 'I've killed you. You're *dead*!'

MacDuff laughed. 'Oh yes,' he said. 'I'm dead. I've been dead for three hundred years. It's your turn now!'

And the axe came down hard on Nobby's skull.

Nobby felt no pain – only a ghastly and unutterable terror, a terror such as he had never felt in his life before. He cowered on the ground, wailing and shivering, and now more of the ghastly things appeared at the mouth of the tunnel: the man in the wheelchair with his headless stump making straight for Nobby's chest . . . and the dog . . . It had run right *through* one of the lamp posts; he could feel its hot breath . . .

Somehow Nobby managed to get to his feet. Then, hitting out with his arms, sobbing, he began to run. He ran faster and faster – away from the ghastly creepy-crawlies that were trying to get him – the vile, unnatural spooks who couldn't really be there . . . only they *were* there . . . they were!

And he ran on and on, out of the fairground, panting and gasping . . . on . . . and on . . . and on . . .

What's more, he never came back again. Not for his car or his belongings or the Tunnel of Hate. Like so many wicked people, he was absolutely petrified of anything he couldn't understand.

'Did you know?' Mr Fisher asked his son, Felix, when it became clear that Nobby was gone for good. 'Did you know that they were ghosts when you asked them to help us out?'

Felix nodded. 'Yes, I did. The first time I was up there Uncle MacDuff ran his wheelchair through me by mistake, and apologized. But I promised not to say anything. You know what it's like when things like that get out: ghost hunters, television crews, people coming to gawp or wanting autographs. Ghosts need their privacy like anybody else.'

'Yes, I see that,' said Mr Fisher. He sighed heavily. 'But oh dear, I shall miss them when they go. It isn't just the money; they were such interesting people. That little girl – I suppose she's a poltergeist?'

'Yes, she is. But I've got good news for you. They've enjoyed themselves so much they say they'll come touring with us for the summer. MacDuff thinks it's good for them to be busy; after all, they've been around for an awfully long time – ever since the cattle raiders came over the border and massacred the family, and that was hundreds of years ago. They said to tell you they'll be perfectly happy travelling on the lorries – they always like to be invisible at night; they sleep better that way.'

So the MacDuffs travelled with the fair and the ghost train made a lot of money and everyone was happy except Nobby Fell, who got picked up by the police a month later for breaking and entering.

As for the Tunnel of Hate, it was towed away and sold for scrap, which was just as well. Making a tunnel out of hate is not a good idea.

HELTER-SKELTER

by **Gillian Cross**
illustrated by **Emma Chichester Clark**

The moment Douglas came out of school he knew the fair had arrived. He could see the helter-skelter.

It was four streets away, in Centenary Park, but it was taller than all the houses in between, towering above the dirty roofs in a glorious cone of green and yellow and blue. Around the cone was a long twisting slide, painted bright scarlet and picked out in gold. Douglas stopped to stare at it.

Coral came charging through the school gates and bumped into him.

'Custard-brain!' she said. 'What are you *doing*?'

'Just looking,' Douglas said gruffly. He felt his face turn red.

Coral gave him a sharp look. Then she glanced over his shoulder and saw the helter-skelter.

'Hey, it's here!' she shrieked. 'Look, everyone! The fair's here! Who's coming down to the park tonight?'

Before Douglas could move, he found himself in the middle of a huge crowd of children, all pointing at the helter-skelter and laughing and making plans.

25

'Let's meet at half past five,' Coral said eagerly. 'In front of the helter-skelter.' She grinned at Douglas. 'I've got to go past your house. I'll call for you at twenty past five?'

I'm not coming, Douglas wanted to say. But he wasn't brave enough. He gave a feeble grin and pushed his way out of the crowd.

As he went down the road, he was shaking and by the time he got home he was feeling weak and strange. He hoped that his mother would send him straight to bed.

But she didn't. As he walked in, he smelt bacon frying and she called from the kitchen.

'Coral just phoned. She says she'll call for you at ten to five instead of twenty past. So I thought I'd better get your tea.'

Douglas went into the kitchen. 'Actually, I don't feel very –'

But his mother wasn't listening. 'I'll have mine with you. I've got the PTA committee coming round at six.'

'I think I'm ill,' Douglas said.

His mother felt his forehead. 'You'll be fine,' she said briskly. 'You just need a bit of fresh air.'

'I could go to bed. I wouldn't be in the way of your committee.'

'Don't be silly.' His mother lifted the bacon on to a plate and cracked a couple of eggs into the frying pan. 'You'll be really sorry if you miss the fair.'

Douglas watched her pile bacon, beans and an

egg on to his plate and he wondered how he was going to eat it. He felt sick.

The food tasted like old rubber. As he chewed it, he could hear the fairground sounds at the end of the road – that unmistakable hurdy-gurdy music and the noise of shouting voices.

'*Roll up, roll up! All the fun of the fair!*'

'*Win yourself a coconut! Six goes for a pound!*'

If he stepped out of the front door, he would see it all. The hoopla stalls and the tombolas, the dodgems and the carousel with the prancing horses.

And the helter-skelter, towering over everything, with its twisting scarlet slide.

Coral came five minutes early, looking very excited. 'There are loads of us meeting down there,' she said, 'and we're going to go on *everything*!'

Douglas's mother reached for her handbag. 'Here,' she said. She pressed a five pound note into Douglas's hand. 'Take this. And win me a teddy bear.'

'Thank you,' Douglas mumbled.

He followed Coral down the path. She was chattering eagerly.

'What shall we do first? Carousel? Dodgems? Or what about the helter-skelter?'

'Dodgems,' Douglas said quickly.

He wasn't usually so decisive. Coral looked round at him.

'The dodgems are great,' Douglas said. 'If we go early, we can all go on at once.'

That convinced Coral. 'OK, everyone,' she said when they met the others. 'Dodgems first! Before they get too crowded.'

The man in charge of the dodgems didn't look too pleased to see a whole crowd of children coming together.

'No bumping,' he said as they scrambled into the cars. 'Or I'll stop the ride.'

'Huh!' Coral muttered. 'Everyone *always* bumps on the dodgems.'

She jumped into the same car as Douglas and took the wheel. Normally that would have annoyed him, but this time he had more to worry about. What were they going to do after the dodgems?

For a few moments he yelled, like the others, while Coral steered the car around, bumping everyone she could reach. Then, when he thought their turn was nearly finished, he twisted sideways and shouted in her ear.

'There's the candyfloss stall! We've got to have candyfloss.'

Coral nodded. As the dodgems slowed down, she jumped out of the car and called to the others.

'Candyfloss next!'

Getting the candyfloss took quite a long time because there were twelve of them. As the candyfloss woman twisted the sticks round in the machine, gathering up pink, sticky fluff, Douglas worked out what to do after that.

'Let's go and watch the fire-eater,' he said.

The fire-eater was performing in an open space just beyond the candyfloss stall. He took a swig of something from a bottle, lit a match and blew a great stream of fire into the air. They stood round him while they ate their candyfloss, throwing pennies into his hat to get him to do it again. And again. And again.

Douglas hardly saw it. *What next?* he was thinking.

By the time the candyfloss was finished, he had the answer. He licked his fingers and wiped them on a tissue. 'Can we go to the rifle range?' he said. 'I've got to win my mum a teddy.'

Coral twitched the tissue out of his hand, dried her own fingers on it and tossed it in a bin. 'Bet you can't,' she said. 'It's really difficult – hitting those little ducks.'

Douglas was counting on that. He wanted to spend a long, long time at the rifle range. He led the way there and paid a pound for five shots.

A procession of yellow plastic ducks was moving slowly across the back of the stall on a conveyor belt, and he squinted along the rifle at them. The rifle sights seemed to be pretty crooked. *Good*, he thought.

'Hit three ducks and win a teddy,' the man in charge said wearily. He looked harassed and exhausted.

'Looks as though he's been up all night,' Coral hissed in Douglas's ear. 'Do you think the baby kept him awake?'

There was a pushchair parked to one side of the rifle range. In it was a baby girl in a fluffy pink jacket. She was holding a greasy bag of chips and coughing miserably. Douglas wondered if it was the smoke from the rifles that made her cough.

Sorry, little girl, he thought as he got ready to fire. *I think I'm going to be firing quite a lot of these*. He was pretty sure that he could waste a lot of time trying to hit ducks. Maybe the others would get bored and wander off while he was shooting. Then he could sneak home on his own.

But it wasn't his lucky day. His very first shot hit a duck. Coral let out a whoop and all the others crowded round, nudging him and hissing advice.

'Go for that one, Doug. Look, it's leaning sideways already.'

'No, try the one behind.'

'Aim a bit to the left.'

He managed to miss with his second and third attempts, but the rifle sights were so crooked that it was hard to know where the shots would go. He aimed the fourth one at a gap between two ducks.

The ball veered off to the right and knocked over a completely different duck.

There was no chance of getting rid of Coral and the others now. They were much too excited. He fired the last shot at random.

Another duck toppled over.

The stallholder yawned wearily and reached down a huge pink teddy. 'Tell everyone where you won it,' he said. 'Please. I need a bit more business.'

Douglas had to take the teddy. He felt really stupid carrying it. It was so big that he couldn't see where he was going. Before he knew what was happening, Coral had seized his shoulder.

'*Now* we're going on the helter-skelter!' she said. 'Come on, everyone!'

Before Douglas could say anything, he was carried away in the rush. The others swept him along with them, pushing and laughing, and it was all he could do to keep his footing. Clutching the pink teddy bear to his chest, he stumbled with them, frantically thinking up excuses.

As they reached the helter-skelter, he began to pull back, shaking his head.

'I can't get up there, can I? Not with this teddy. I'll wait for you down here.'

'Rubbish!' Coral pulled the teddy out of his hands and thrust it at the helter-skelter man. 'You'll take care of this, won't you?'

'Certainly will, darling.' The man gave her a gap-toothed grin and pushed the teddy into the hut behind him. 'It'll be quite safe with me. You go on up and enjoy yourselves.'

Coral dropped her money into his hand, took a mat and walked into the helter-skelter. As soon as she was through the doorway, Douglas stepped back and gasped dramatically.

'Oh – I can't come. I haven't got any money left!'

Coral stuck her head back through the doorway. 'Don't be silly. Your mum gave you five pounds.'

Drat. She'd seen that, of course. 'Must have dropped some,' Douglas muttered.

'You idiot!' Coral said impatiently. She pulled some money out of her pocket and gave it to the helter-skelter man. 'I'll pay for him too.'

Douglas still hung back. Coral peered at him.

'You're not *scared*, are you?' she said sharply.

'Of course not,' Douglas lied.

The others were pushing at his back, wanting to get inside the helter-skelter. He couldn't escape. Miserably, he took his mat and went through the door.

It was even worse than he had expected. The inside of the helter-skelter was dark and airless with steep wooden ladders zigzagging up to the top. Up and up and up. There were no windows and nothing to let in light except the opening at the top. Reluctantly, Douglas stepped on to the first ladder, clutching his mat in one hand and holding on with the other.

Immediately, he was trapped. The ladder in front of him was crowded with people moving slowly and blocking his way. There were more people coming up behind, pushing impatiently. Douglas kept his eyes on the ladder and climbed steadily, trying not to think.

There were four ladders altogether, to reach the top. They slanted from side to side of the helter-skelter tower, with little platforms in between them to let people change from one ladder to another.

That was the worst part. Changing ladders. By the time Douglas reached the top of the last one, he was sweating and shaking and his heart was thudding like a drum. He pulled himself through the doorway and out on to the platform at the very top of the helter-skelter.

And he saw the fair spread out below him.

It was a sickening moment. He clung to the side of the doorway, terrified that he would fall off and crash to the ground if he moved any further. In front of him was the beginning of the twisting scarlet slide. Coral was sitting at the top of it, holding on to the side wall with both hands and lifting herself up so that the woman in charge could slip her mat underneath her.

As Douglas stopped in the doorway, she glanced back for a second. Her eyes widened when she saw his face and he knew that he must look as bad as he felt.

'*Doug!*' she said. 'You should have –'

But she never finished. The helter-skelter woman put a hand in the middle of her back and pushed lightly.

'Off you go!' she said.

Automatically, Coral let go and slid away, sweeping round the corner and out of sight.

'Next,' said the helter-skelter woman.

Desperately, Douglas clung to the side of the

doorway. His head was spinning. He couldn't face taking the two steps to the top of the slide, let alone sliding down it. But how else could he get down? The ladders behind him were crammed with people. He would never be able to get past them if he tried to climb down that way.

And anyway, climbing down the inside of the helter-skelter seemed almost as frightening as sliding round the outside.

Vaguely, he was aware of the woman's voice, trying to persuade him to move.

'. . . come along now . . . not as bad as you think . . . you won't see a thing once you've started . . . just take a look . . .'

Douglas forced his eyes open. The woman was pointing at the slide, trying to get him to look down it. But, instead, his eyes were drawn to the fair below him. And the terrible drop . . .

Everything looked very tiny and very far down. He could see it all. The dodgems. The candyfloss stall and the fire-eater. The rifle stall. It was all horribly, horribly clear and he couldn't stop looking.

He saw the fire-eater take his next swig from the bottle. He saw him light a match and blow. And he saw a couple of teenage boys pick up a tissue from the ground and laugh as they threw it into the air. Towards the plume of fire.

'. . . you can't stay here forever . . .' the helter-skelter woman was saying. '. . . you'll have to move . . .'

But Douglas couldn't move. And so he saw the tissue float up and up, trapped in the draught of hot air. It touched the fire and the boys laughed as it burst into flame. Then – as the fire-eater turned to yell at them – the flames went out and it began drifting down again, smouldering at the edges.

And it fell into the pushchair beside the rifle stall.

'Look!' Douglas croaked. 'Look! The baby – the pushchair –'

But his mouth was dry and he couldn't get more words out. And the helter-skelter woman wasn't listening anyway. She was pulling at his arm, trying to get him to let go of the doorway and take his turn.

'Come on, now. You can't just block everyone else. Don't be silly.'

'B-but –' Douglas stuttered. 'You've got to – someone's got to –'

But there wasn't time to explain. And, anyway, what could the helter-skelter woman do? No one would hear if she yelled from up here. Someone had to go down. And there was only one way down . . .

It wasn't really a decision. He just let go of the doorway and launched himself forward, flinging himself full length on to the slide, with the mat clutched to his chest. He heard the woman's protesting voice – 'You can't do it like that!' – and then he was away, sweeping round the corner.

And round and round and round.

It wasn't frightening at all, because the sides of

the slide were so high. All he could see was bright red wood on one side and a swirl of green and yellow and blue on the other. But he hardly had time to take that in. He was concentrating on keeping his legs and arms in the air, so that he could get down as quickly as possible.

The moment he hit the cushion at the bottom, he was on his feet. Coral was at his elbow, shouting in his ear.

'Doug! Are you all right? Why didn't you *say* –?'

He just shook her off and ran. It was still twenty metres to the rifle stall and he felt like a snail as he raced towards it, bumping into people and shoving them out of the way.

By the time he reached the pushchair, he had no breath left to speak. He could see the smouldering tissue lying on the blanket round the baby's legs. The blanket was beginning to scorch and turn brown – and only a few millimetres away was the baby's bag of chips. She was holding the greasy paper just where the flames were going to start. At any moment –

'Fire!' yelled Douglas. He threw himself at the pushchair and grabbed the blanket, bundling it up and tearing it away from the baby.

Immediately, she began to cry.

'Here!' The stallholder turned round furiously. 'What d'you think you're doing? You leave her alone!'

Douglas was sure that the stallholder was going to

hit him, but all he could do was double up, gasping and gasping for breath.

It was Coral who did the talking. She was close behind him and she flung herself at the stallholder, thumping his chest with both her fists.

'Don't be so *stupid*! Douglas wouldn't do something like that unless he had a *reason*! Can't you see the state he's in? Can't you *see*?'

And then the blanket started to smoke. Grey wisps snaked their way out of the scorched material and the smell was finally strong enough to overcome the smell of the rifle smoke.

The stallholder went a sickly green and lunged for the baby. He wrenched the straps undone and clasped her to his chest, hugging her fiercely.

'A tissue!' Douglas panted. 'The fire-eater – some boys – I was up the helter-skelter –'

'He saved her life!' Coral said fiercely. 'Don't you see? He saved your baby's life.'

The stallholder hugged the baby harder. Then he looked apologetically at Douglas. 'Sorry, mate. Anything I can do to say thank you? Want a teddy bear for your mum?'

'I've got one, thanks,' Douglas said quickly.

'Well, you ought to have something. Here.' The man shifted the baby on to his hip and fumbled in his pocket. 'Here.' He held out a coin to Douglas. 'Have another go on the helter-skelter. You can't have enjoyed the last one much.'

Douglas went pale, but Coral had already twitched

the coin out of the man's hand. 'Thanks a lot. Come on, Doug.' She marched off towards the helter-skelter.

Douglas went running after her. 'I don't *want* another go.' Somehow it was quite easy to say that now. 'It scares me stiff.'

'That's why you've got to do it,' Coral said easily. 'Come on.'

This time the helter-skelter was almost empty. Douglas climbed the ladders with his mat under his arm and thought, *I could be anywhere. In the gym at school, or halfway up Mount Everest*. He could hear Coral's feet on the ladder behind him and he kept in step with her, climbing fast.

When they came out at the top, the helter-skelter woman looked horrified.

'Not you again! Now if there's any fuss –'

'No fuss,' Douglas said. It was hard to speak evenly, because his heart was thudding again, but he made himself let go of the door frame. It would look pretty stupid if he couldn't slide down this time. He had to do it.

Coral was close behind him as he lowered himself on to the slide.

'Here!' she said. 'Don't forget this.'

She dumped the pink teddy into his lap.

Douglas was still wondering how she'd managed to climb the ladders with a mat *and* a giant teddy when the helter-skelter woman planted a hand in the middle of his back.

'Off you go!' she said. 'Nothing to be afraid of.'

And there wasn't. All Douglas could see was the pink teddy grinning into his face. And he grinned back.

All

      the

           way

                down

                      the

                            helter-skelter.

GOLDFISH

by Joyce Dunbar
illustrated by Polly Dunbar

Did you know that a goldfish swimming round a bowl has a memory so short that each time round is like the first time ever? Did you know that a goldfish swimming round a bowl has a memory so short that each time round is like the first time ever? Did you know that a goldfish swimming round a bowl has a memory so short that each time round is like the first time ever? Did you know that a goldfish swimming round

GOING STRAIGHT

by **Kaye Umansky**
illustrated by **Quentin Blake**

Imagine it. Midnight in an empty fairground. A black velvet sky, thickly sprinkled with cold, bright stars. The swings hang still. The hulking ferris wheel stands silent. Over on the carousel, the painted horses hang suspended from their golden poles – stiff, lifeless and gleaming. And then . . .

The eye of the pink horse moved in its socket. At the same time, the red horse's tail swished and the purple horse twitched an ear. Then the green horse pawed the air with its hoof, the yellow horse snorted down its nose and the blue horse shook its mane and said, gloomily: 'Well, here we all are again, then. Another day of going round in circles and getting nowhere.'

'Yep.' The green horse gave a little snort. 'You said it. Day in, day out, up, down, round an' round, chasin' each other's backsides. Funny old world. But, hey! It's a job.'

'Yeah,' said the blue horse. 'It's a *job*.' But it didn't sound convinced.

'What we were made for, innit? Goin' round in circles,' observed the red horse, cheerily. 'Done it for years. That's what we do. That's why we *are*.'

'Still,' said the blue horse.

There was a pause then, while everyone concentrated on flexing legs, shaking out stiff joints and getting more comfortable on the poles.

'Stars are low tonight,' remarked the pink horse, after a bit. 'Looks like we're in for a frost. They'll be taking us off to the warehouse for the winter refit soon, I shouldn't wonder. Can't say I'll be sorry. Can't take the cold like I used to.'

'Me neither,' agreed the purple horse. 'I'm certainly ready for an overhaul. That crack in my neck's been giving me gyp lately.'

'I'm desperate for a paint job,' sighed the yellow horse. 'And my tail needs replacing.'

'You're right there,' observed green, from directly behind. 'You're not exactly a pretty sight. From the back.'

'Mustn't grumble, though,' said red. 'We're all getting on a bit, but at least we're still working. Eh? At least they haven't replaced us with motorbikes.'

'*Yet*,' said blue, meaningfully.

There was an uncomfortable little silence.

'You shouldn't talk like that,' muttered yellow. 'It's bad luck. Talking like that.'

'I'm just saying,' said blue.

'Let's talk about something else,' said purple. 'Let's

moan about the music. Are they ever going to change that flipping tune?'

'I've got a better idea. Let's complain about the kids,' suggested yellow.

'What, *again*?' sighed blue, rolling its eyes to the heavens. But it was in the minority. Complaining about the kids was what they did every night. That, and look at the stars.

'Good idea!' said red, happily. 'I'll start. Kids today. Huh!' It blew down its nose for emphasis and stamped on the air.

'They don't improve, that's for sure,' said yellow, right on cue. 'Getting worse, if anything. I had a right little horror on today, did you see him? The one in the baseball hat? With the boots?'

'Kick, did he?' asked purple, sympathetically.

'I'll say. Felt like kicking him back. Took a whacking great chip out of my side, see?'

'I can't see your side,' said pink, straining on its pole. 'Not from where I am.'

'I can,' said the green horse. 'It's nasty.'

'Look on the bright side,' advised red. 'They'll *have* to paint you now. Anyway, *you're* complaining? I got a screamer. Let rip the minute the music started up. Right in my ear it was.' The red horse raised its voice an octave to mimic its panicked rider. '*Waaaaaa! Mumeeeee! Lemme orrrrrffff!* Did my head in.'

'It's the ones with the candyfloss I can't bear,' said purple, with a theatrical little shudder. 'Those hands! Those horrible, sticky little *hands*.'

'And then they poke the stick up your nose when they get off,' agreed yellow. 'I've got one up there now from last week. Along with the rest of the old rubbish they post up my nostrils.'

'At least you've never had one throw up all over you,' said green, bitterly. 'Remember what happened to me that time?'

There was a short, reverent pause while everyone thought deeply about what had happened to the green horse that time.

'What I want to know is, where have all the nice, quiet little girls gone?' mused the pink horse. 'The ones who sit still and wave at their mummies and daddies and kiss your nose when they get off? Don't see many of them around these days. When you do, they never choose me. In fact, nobody's been choosing me lately. Why, I wonder?'

'Probably something to do with the dirty great nail sticking up out of your saddle, dear,' said purple.

'*Really?*' Pink was very surprised. 'Well! And I never knew. Why didn't you tell me?'

'I thought you'd rather not know.'

'Of course I want to know. I thought they'd just gone off pink.'

'I never get the quiet ones,' grumbled yellow. 'I always get the kickers. Kids. They don't improve. Getting worse, if anything.'

'You've said that already,' remarked the blue horse, rather snappishly.

'So?'

'So I'm saying. Even when we *talk*, we go round in circles. I don't want to hear about kids any more. That's all we ever do, moan about kids and go round in circles.'

There was a little silence. After a bit, the green horse said, 'That's life, eh? A rat race.'

'Well, in our case, a horse race,' corrected red, adding, 'but I get your point.'

'Main thing is to keep cheerful.'

'Oh yes, got to keep cheerful.'

'Circles!' groaned blue. It was clear that it didn't want to be cheerful. Morosely, it pawed the air. 'Up and down. Round and round. Round and round and round and round and round and round –'

The horses caught each other's eyes and exchanged meaningful looks. The blue horse was a bit moody, with an up-and-down sort of personality. For the last few nights it hadn't talked much, which was a bad sign.

'You're blue tonight,' said green. Everyone stared at the blue horse, which had its head bent and was muttering '. . . round an' round an' round . . .' under its breath.

'Yeah,' said red. 'What's up?'

'. . . an' up an' down an' up an' down an' up down updownupdownupdown . . .'

'Come on. Spit it out,' encouraged the red horse. 'You're among friends.'

'I dunno,' sighed the blue horse. 'Sometimes I wish life wasn't quite so – *circular*. Always coming back to where we started. Always knowing what's ahead.'

'Red's flaky backside,' observed the purple horse. 'That's what's ahead of me.'

'Bit of a bum view,' remarked yellow. It was an old joke, but they laughed anyway.

All except for the blue horse, who said, 'I just feel there might be something good we're missing.'

'Like what?' asked the red horse.

'I dunno. Wonderful things. You know. Outside the carousel. Beyond the fairground. Somewhere else. I dunno. Am I making sense?'

The horses eyed each other uneasily. They weren't used to this kind of talk.

'It's just a mood,' ventured the red horse, kindly. 'It'll pass.'

'Will it, though?' The blue horse raised its head towards the starry sky. 'Oh, I know what we do is all right *really*. Well, of course, we *moan*. Who doesn't? But we give people fun and that's *good*. And you guys – well, I couldn't ask for a better circle of friends. It's just . . . ' It gave a little sigh. 'It's the going round. That's what's getting to me. Just for once, I wish we could go straight.'

And just at that very minute, something wonderful happened. A star shot across the sky. It travelled straight as an arrow, trailing a tail of silver sparks in its wake. Then it winked out. The whole event took less than a second.

'See that?' said the red horse. 'See the shooter?'

'Supposed to make a wish,' said pink. 'That's what I heard, anyway.'

'Just an old mare's tale,' said the yellow horse. 'Wishing on a star. What were we talking about again?'

'Hey,' said the blue horse. There was a certain edge to its voice. 'Hey, you lot!'

'Kids,' said pink. 'I was saying you don't get many nice little g–'

'*Hey, you lot!*' said blue again, more urgently this time.

'What?' asked pink, slightly irritable now.

'Is it just me,' said the blue horse, slowly, 'or has my pole come loose? Where it joins the saddle?'

'Don't be daft,' said green. 'That's impossible. They always check 'em. Safety, ain't it? No way the poles can come loo–'

It broke off. Its eyes widened in disbelief.

The blue horse was no longer attached to its pole! It had moved away from the circular platform and was floating in the air – all on its own! It bobbed about a bit, dipped, rose again, then landed gently with all four hooves resting on the trampled grass.

'See?' said the blue horse, triumphantly. 'Look! I'm not hanging, I'm standing! All by myself!'

'How did you do that?' gasped red, staring wide-eyed at the blue horse, then back at the empty pole.

'I wished, didn't I?' said the blue horse. 'You heard me. I wished we could go straight, just as the star went shooting. And now we can! Come on, try it! It's easy!'

'He's right, you know!' said yellow, excitely. 'My

pole's loose too; I can feel it. Hang on, let's just see what happens if I . . .!'

And, with a little wriggle, it too sailed off its pole.

The remaining horses stared, open-mouthed and wide-eyed. Then they too gave nervous little wriggles – and one by one they floated off the golden poles!

They experimented a bit, getting the feel of what it was like to be free and unattached. They examined one another from all sides. They floated up to each other and touched noses. Each was interested to observe what the others looked like from the front.

Each privately thought that everyone else looked decidedly old and worse for wear.

Finally, they turned in the air and floated in a straight line, shoulder to shoulder, facing the strangely empty carousel.

'Our home,' said yellow, wonderingly. 'So *that's* what it looks like from the outside. Shabbier than I thought. Some of the lights have come loose at the top, see? At least they ought to get those mended.'

'Look at the peeling paint. You don't realize until you stand back from it, do you?' mused the green horse.

'Of course, it looks a lot worse without us,' said red. 'No point in a carousel without horses, is there?'

'It looks rubbish,' agreed green. 'Just a big, old, useless round thing. Like a fish bowl without any fish in it.'

'So are we gonna stay here talking all night, or what?' said the blue horse. It pawed the ground and gave an impatient snort. 'We're pole-less, we're fancy free, and the sky's the limit! Now, we've got options. The way I see it, we can bunch up in a group or string out neck to neck, or fly in a tidy line.'

'Tidy line,' said the pink horse, promptly. 'It's what we're used to. And we need to stick together. We don't want to lose each other.'

'Agreed,' said the blue horse. 'Everyone line up behind me.'

'Why you?' objected purple. 'How come you're the leader? And don't say you're always in front on the carousel, because we *all* think that. We have to think differently if we're going straight.'

'Who made the wish?' argued the blue horse, slightly sulky. But it saw the purple horse's point. Going straight did require a new sort of thinking.

'I think we should all take a turn,' said the yellow horse. 'That's fair.'

'How can we take turns if we're going straight?' asked green, confused.

In the end, they reached a compromise. They would fly in a line, taking turns to be leader. Blue horse would lead first because, as it so rightly pointed out, it had made the wish. They would also vary the order they flew in, because it would be a novelty to follow a different-coloured tail.

'Ready?' said the blue horse, when they were finally in position.

'Ready,' chorused the others, pawing the ground and snorting.

'Just one small point,' added green.

'What?'

'If we go straight – *really* straight – and carry on going, where do we end up? And how will we get back?'

'Who knows?' said blue. 'Who cares? We might not even bother to come back. We might end up somewhere we like better. Come on. Reach for the stars!'

And it reared up on its hind legs, then rose gently, gracefully, into the air. Behind, in a tidy line, the others did the same.

Up they went, until they were higher than the tall fence surrounding the fairground. Higher still they rose, until they were looking down on the carousel. And now, they were higher than the ferris wheel. Higher than the trees. Below, dark fields stretched out on all sides. Above was the sky. And straight ahead was the North Star.

They aimed for that.

Early the following morning, two men – one tall, one short – stood contemplating the carousel. There was a thick ground frost. Their breath hung in the air.

'. . . and that's just 'ow I found it, boss,' the short one was saying. 'Every last one of 'em gone. Got to be an inside job. No signs of a break-in. And whoever done it 'ad the right tools, as well as the know-how, to get 'em off the poles.'

'Mm,' said the tall man, thoughtfully, rubbing his chin.

'Another thing. 'Ow did they get 'em out? You'd need a lorry to shift that lot, but both gates were padlocked.'

'Mm.'

'What I don't get is . . . *why*?' continued the short man. 'I mean, what good are a load of clapped-out old carousel horses to anyone? Old fashioned, ain't they? Kids want somethin' more modern these days. Motorbikes an' that. Matter o' fact, I was gonna say to you, no point in keepin' 'em for another season.

In a way, whoever nicked 'em done us a favour. Whole carousel needs scrappin' . . .'

But the fairground boss wasn't listening. He was thinking of something his small, over-imaginative daughter had said to him over the breakfast table in the caravan. Something about a dream she had had. Something about getting up in the night and glancing out the window at the stars – and seeing a line of painted horses flying across the sky – undeviating, straight as an arrow, straight as a die.

Did they reach the North Star? That, I don't know. But I do know that they saw wonderful things on the way.

THE LITTLE DOG LAUGHED

by **Geraldine McCaughrean**
illustrated by **Michael Foreman**

I think my blood must be frozen, because I cannot move. Not a finger. Poor Mother. Bad winter. First her accident. And now me. I never wanted to come here, but how could I refuse? If you had seen Mother's face, you would have come, and you're not even family.

When the Thames turned to jelly on Christmas Day, it seemed like a magic trick. The jelly set. First the surface crusted over, then the water under it. Lightermen poked about with staves. Mudlarks, finding the mudflats hard as iron, tottered out on to the river, clutching their pails and bits of stick. Within the day, boys were daring each other, young men trying to impress their girls. Soon whole families were out there, skating arm in arm; bands of office clerks, and watermen put out of work by the frost.

By New Year the Thames was a smooth, solid causeway, white as white between the dirty buildings on either bank. If you looked closely, of course, it was filthy – rope ends, newspapers, broken barrels, clods of tar, dog mess, dead cats and rats and pigeons. But Londoners looked out and saw only this amazing white highway splitting the city in two. There was a holiday mood.

'You can always sell to a holiday crowd,' Mother said. 'Happy people buy.' And she was right. Before long, all kinds of booths sprang up on the ice – hawkers selling sweets and mittens and journals – even a man with a hot-chestnut stand. Mother loaded every piece of work she had into a basket and we went and stood on the river too.

The cold struck up through my feet, and if I held still too long the sacking round my shoes stuck to the ice as if it had been glued. Our steamy breath condensed and froze on our eyelashes and lips. But we did a good steady trade. It was as if time had stopped flowing, along with the river, and people were no longer thinking about saving for tomorrow's rent or the grocery bill or against bad times. They bought skates for their children and scarves for themselves. They drank mulled ale to warm their hands and their insides. They even bought pencil sketches of themselves standing in the middle of the Thames, to prove to their children they had been there, at the Frost Fair of 1740.

And we were there too – Mother and I – selling ribbons and scarves and caps, turning a profit, doing all right for a widow woman and her short-sighted daughter.

Then it melted.

The crowds were smaller that day: I suppose the

rich people had barometers and knew the weather was changing. The only difference I had noticed was that the ice was more slippery; it was easier to fall over.

That is what happened to Mother. On our way down the steps, she slipped and fell three yards on to the ice below. People crowded round. Someone said 'collarbone'. Someone else said 'arm'. Either way, her working hand was out of use. I could see her reckoning up the disaster. In our house we almost keep count in millinery. Mother breaking her arm was a 23-hat, mile-long-ribbon of a misfortune.

'You do it, Lily,' she said, righting the spilled basket with her foot. 'Gather up the stock before it spoils. And don't come home till it's all sold . . . You there! Get your great boot off my caps!'

So while Mother was carried home on someone's living-room chair, I dragged the basket out into the middle of the river and hoped that everyone bought something and no one asked for change. (Mother had all the small change in her apron pocket.)

At about noon, the ice started to growl like a giant dog. Nearby, a man selling jellied eels said, 'She's melting.' And in a flash, he was gone. So too were the dried flowers and the coffee stand. The man who had been taking bets on his 'Pedigree Racing Rats' headed for the bank, leaving a half-dozen rats scooting fruitlessly up and down runways in the ice.

Fright made things seem to spin – London Bridge, the monuments, the river. The steps in the river wall were crowded with people pushing and struggling to get off the ice. I thought, 'What if I can't get there in time?' And I panicked. When my feet slipped from under me, I ran on hands and feet, splashing up meltwater. It was not until I got home that I saw my fingers were webbed with ice. Ice mermaid.

Mother was still sitting on that borrowed chair, looking green round the gills. 'The frost's melting!' I panted, and my windpipe rattled with ice.

'Where's the basket?' was all she said.

In my panic I had forgotten to pick up the basket with all the caps in it. 'There's a month's work in that basket,' she said, lurching to her feet, pushing me aside. I followed her back to the wharf steps. But there was a lighterman there, with a big stave, who would not let us pass: 'Unsafe. Nobody allowed.'

So we stood on London Bridge and watched the deserted Frost Fair offer its wares to nobody but the bruise-coloured sky. There was a hut with *Old Gold* chalked on its side, a skittle frame, a souvenir booth . . . and, of course, a lone basket of caps and ribbons and scarves. It looked like a little galleon dressed in bunting.

Before nightfall, the ice fractured, and the centre of the Thames came snaking back to life.

Before January was out, though, it refroze. It was not smooth this time. Great chunks of old, grey ice as big as houses jutted up at crazy angles all along both banks, leaving a flat white 'street' down the middle. It was awkward to get out there, but no one was put off:

not the man with the bear, nor the man selling painting lessons, nor the toffee-maker, nor the woman giving donkey rides . . . nor the milliner's daughter with her borrowed basket of second-rate caps. With my bad eyes, and Mother sewing one-handed, it was all we could do to fill a basket. But we had to turn a penny if we were to keep a roof over our heads through the worst winter in living memory. And you can sell anything to a holiday crowd.

By the time the Frost Fair was in full swing again, even I was happy to be there, for all my terror of the river worming by below me. The crowds were immense! Alongside me, a printer was typesetting people's names, inking the letters and printing them on to a souvenir sheet:

THIF IF TO CERTIFY THAT I

Miss Eliza Munday

DID WALK UPON YE RIVER THAMEF

ON THIF 3rd DAY OF FEBRUARY 1740

To my left, there were prizes on offer to whoever could throw a live cat furthest. Behind me, hidden by a press of spectators, dogs were baiting a bear tethered to the ice by a spade anchor. I am glad I could not see it; I do not greatly care for blood sports.

But in front of me – best of all! – was a great tin carousel. It was worked by a man winding a huge handle. As he wound, the brightly painted canopy wobbled and wavered and spun on its pivot, and eight thick ropes swung outwards from its rim. Attached to the ropes by meat-hooks, eight carved wooden coaches tilted and flew through the air in a breathtaking swirl of dazzling colour. In the grey air, under a lowering, grey sky and seen through clouds of my own grey breath, *Mr Caldecott's Wondrous Flying Coaches* seemed to me the most marvellous sight in all London.

Day after day I stood and watched children riding that carousel. Every time he saw me looking, the handle-winder would wink and beckon, but I knew I must not leave Mother's basket. We could not spare the penny, either, for me to ride the Flying Coaches. Even so! It is one marvel to stand on water that has turned stone-hard; it is quite another to fly through the air in a scarlet painted coach!

One day a gentleman came by, bought a muffler, and gave me a sugar lump. I liked the sugar, but I was not so fond of his dog, a grumpy little bull terrier, with feet that turned outwards like an antique chair.

'Don't fear Trump,' said the gentleman. 'He's soft as a bath sponge.'

'I am not feared for myself, sir, but that he should chew on the smoking caps. They cost nine pence apiece.' We both watched the animal's drool trickle over Mother's embroidery. He gave me another sugar lump.

'Do you think Old Trump resembles me?' asked the gentleman. 'People often say how alike we are.'

How can you answer a question like that? 'You both have very good faces, I'm sure,' I said, and curtsied.

'How gracious. Have a sugar lump. Have you ridden the Flying Coaches yet?'

'I have to keep by my basket,' I said.

Just then, there was a roar of laughter, and a ginger cat was thrown across the ice. It tried to get to its feet, but slid into the printer's stall, scattering his trays of letters. The gentleman and I ran to help him gather them up.

They were all backwards, those letters – like reflections of words.

'How I do abhor these bestial, cruel games!' said my gentleman, scowling at the cat throwers.

'Come to paint the fair, Mr Hogarth?' asked the printer respectfully.

'I might, if there was a single place to set my easel,' roared the gentleman. 'The artists are ranged along the Embankment thicker than posts in a fence. Come springtime, there will be enough commemorative masterpieces to make a pontoon bridge over the Thames. I shall paint that, instead.'

'Shall I print your name on a souvenir sheet, Mr Hogarth?' said the printer shyly, as one artist to a much greater one. 'Free of charge, naturally.'

Mr Hogarth thought about this while he rattled another sugar lump around inside his teeth. 'Tell you what! You may print my *dog's* name: TRUMP.' (The printer began picking out the letters with amazing deftness, given the blueness of his fingertips.) '. . . But not on a souvenir sheet. Print it on the ice! Then may we confound the poet who wrote, "*All your better deeds/Shall be in water writ.*" ' And with a twirl of his muffler, Mr Hogarth squatted down and etched in the ice with a little penknife. At first I could see nothing – a grey picture carved in grey ice – but when he wiped it over with the printer's inky rag, there it was: the most perfect little study of a dog's face.

Or, of course, it might have been a self-portrait. Mr Hogarth did look *very* like his dog.

So, after that, I had five things to look at while I stood on the ice selling caps and scarves. I could watch the bear-baiting or the cat-throwing (though I never did); I could watch the printer shaping people's names, or children riding the carousel; or I could look down at Trump, etched on the ice in purple printer's ink alongside his stamped, purple name.

The man winding the carousel must have made a mint of money from the Frost Fair, because one day he winked and beckoned and called over to me: 'Free ride to the little lady with the blue nose!'

So of course I went. Even though that day was the thirteenth. Even though I should have stayed by my basket. Even though Mother was relying on me.

He lifted me into one of the Flying Coaches. I felt sick with excitement. Suddenly the day was not nearly so cold. There was a jolt. We jiggled in our seats. I thought, I'm too heavy. I shan't fly outwards. I shall just dangle here, with my bootlaces dragging on the ice. Then the sky began to spin and I was flying.

There was music from the barrel organ, smells from

the coffee stalls and hot chestnuts, a slew of colours. I shut my eyes. There was laughter and the barking of dogs, a penny whistle and a green sickness under my ribs. I opened my eyes again. There was the printer waving to me – and there was a thief filching from my basket, as fast as a squirrel pouching nuts.

I shouted for the roundabout man to stop winding, but he only laughed, thinking I was scared, and wound even faster. I could hear the rasp of his breath as he sucked icy air into an ailing chest. I wanted to throw myself out, but I seemed to be house-high above the ice, and everything was spinning. I tried to keep track of which way the boy set off when he had finished robbing me. I saw him look back, grin and thumb his nose. Then my toes scuffed the ice and I was down.

'I'll have the ears off you, you thieving little . . .' But when I jumped clear of the coach and set off to run, I found that the whole frozen Thames had become a carousel. The houses on the bridge were waltzing. The ice was sloping under my feet. The stalls and booths along the frozen river had become Flying Coaches. The ride had made me so dizzy that I fell flat, my face landing almost on top of Mr Hogarth's ice engraving.

I waited for the giddiness to pass, looking down at Trump's portrait, and Trump looked back at me. That is when he smiled. The dog began to smile! It was no more than I deserved – to be jeered at by a cartoon dog – but I was not imagining it. The ice beneath was pushing upwards, distorting the engraving, as the River Thames flexed her thawing muscles.

'*The ice is moving!*' I pulled myself to my feet, but the printer had gone to buy his lunch.

'*The ice is moving!*' I shouted in the direction of the carousel. The roundabout man laughed, thinking I was still dizzy from the ride. I shouted again, but he could not hear me above the music and his own rasping breaths. A new party of children had clambered aboard the Flying Coaches and already the tin canopy was starting to spin.

I think the bear heard me. Or perhaps it felt the movement through the pads of its leathery feet: they say brute beasts can sense danger. Anyway, as I stood there, the crowd of baiters and gamblers scattered, and this black bear came running on all fours, dragging the spade anchor behind it. (The thaw must have loosed the anchor.) It looked happy, startled by its sudden freedom, bounding and gambolling over the ice on claws that gripped like hobnails. The dogs chasing after it were far more frightening. The blood on their masks made me run blindly back, not looking where I was going. The roundabout, turning at full speed now, swung out its coaches, and the corner of one must have struck me on the temple, because I went down like a dead thing.

When I came to, the river was deserted. A litter of hats and gloves and broadsheets and apple cores and booths remained, and among the great craggy outcrops of ice I could see the backs of a few people still clambering ashore.

Mr Caldecott's Wondrous Flying Coaches teetered drunkenly over me, one side of its tin canopy resting on the ice, its coaches hanging anyhow, like lynched men. The other booths were undulating gently, like ships at anchor. Then the fairground broke up like a biscuit. Islands of ice jostled each other for elbow room. And everything – all of it – moved gently downstream. The leaning ramshackle houses on London Bridge, with their bulging windows, seemed to boggle in disbelief, as if the river were some monster waking from sleep.

Near at hand, an artist's easel walked a few crabbing steps and fell into the water. Seagulls squabbled over a half-eaten bun. Far in the distance, on an island of its own, the bear was still dragging the anchor about by its chain. Next time I looked, it was gone.

At least Mother's borrowed basket was still in reach. I gathered up anything I could – any abandoned valuables – and crammed them into the basket. They might make up for the things stolen by that wretched thief. I knew I ought to try and jump ashore, using the ice fragments for stepping stones. But as I tried to plot a route to the stone stairs in the Embankment wall, the stairs and the Embankment and London itself all moved away to stern, and the channels grew too wide to leap.

With a tinny crumpling, *Mr Caldecott's Wondrous Flying Coaches* slumped over and slid off the ice and into deep, black, weltering water. A few seconds later, one of the coaches must have floated free of its hook, because it burst to the surface like a scarlet whale.

The water licked the ice transparent, so that I could see the moving darkness below me. Somewhere down there, the bear had gone back to its fairground calling, tethered by its anchor to the riverbed, fighting off dogfish and eels.

People too.

I tried to spread my weight over my shrinking lilypad of ice, but water closed over it from all sides, cold as shearing blades. Then it just . . . shrugged me off.

I've seen a shelled egg turn white as it slips into a pan of water. I was that egg. The water turned me white with cold: my heart, my skin, my brain, my thoughts – white. All I could think was to pull myself aboard this scarlet coach.

So here I am, coaching down the Thames highway, icepeaks for my skyline and drowned men's hats bobbing about me like outriders. I think my blood must be frozen, because I cannot move. Not a finger.

Wapping Pierhead is crowded with people – Wapping Stairs, too – gapers and gawpers and people pointing. There's Mother, her arm in a sling. Come to see what's become of her profits and her borrowed basket.

At least, I suppose that's why she is crying.

I am sorry, Mother. The carousel was so pretty: I was tempted. So sorry.

A bargepole? Ow! Caught in my hair and pulling. Ice still solid as stone here. Stone wall as cold as ice. 'I regret: I don't think I can, sir. My hands, see? Too cold. Oh, Mr Hogarth, sir! Don't *you* come down, sir! *You* shouldn't come down Wapping Stairs, sir, not in that suit! Shoes will be ruined! No, I can't let go of the basket. Me and this basket, we're one. Well, yes. If you would be so kind. I'll follow you up when the feeling comes back to my legs, sir. Oh! Take particular care of the caps, if you please, sir. You don't know my mother the way I do.'

I'll just sit here on the steps for a moment and watch my scarlet coach, tumbling onwards, lickety-split, and nothing to stop it between here and the sea.

WE'RE GOING TO THE FAIR

by John Foster
illustrated by Tony Ross

We're going to the fair!
We're going to the fair!

What will we do at the fair tonight?
What will we do at the fair?

We'll ride round and round on the roundabout.
Round, round, round.
We'll whirl and spin on the big wheel
High above the ground.

We'll whizz down the helter-skelter.
Slide, slide, slide.
We'll look at the House of Horrors,
But we won't go inside.

We'll swing to and fro on the swinging boats.
Swing, swing, swing.
We'll hook the ducks and win a prize –
A monkey on a string.

We'll ride in the dark on the ghost train.
Scream! Scream! Scream!
We'll buy a stick of candyfloss
And a huge ice cream.

That's what we'll do at the fair tonight.
That's what we'll do at the fair.

LEFT, KLUNK! LEFT, KLUNK!

by **Jeremy Strong**
illustrated by **Korky Paul**

It was an extraordinary piece of workmanship. There were fifteen soldiers in the marching band and the fat conductor up at the front. The fat conductor held a long mace, which he lifted and lowered in time to the music, while his little legs marched beneath his big fat belly, left, right, left right!

Behind the conductor came the fifteen musicians. First there were two flautists, then two clarinettists. They were followed by a pair of trumpeters, two horn players, two trombonists, two snare drummers, a brace of big bass drummers and a cymbal player.

The little carousel was wound up with a metal key and off they went, while the music box slowly unwound, tinkling its pretty marching tune. Round and round went the soldiers, with their legs bravely snapping out, left, right, left, right. The conductor lifted his mace, the musicians blew and banged their instruments and the music box went ping, ping, ting-a-ding!

The toymaker was delighted with his work. He wound up the carousel over and over again. He placed it in the front of his shop window, so that the passing world would see just what fine toys he could make. Round and round went the soldiers, left, right, left, right, and the music box went ping, ping, ting-a-ding!

But, what the toymaker could not see was that there was trouble amongst the fine soldiers. Maybe they were only a few centimetres tall, but they had big feelings, and one of the snare drummers didn't like being kicked up the backside. Every time a big bass drummer behind shot out his right foot, he kicked the snare drummer right up the bottom – *Bumff!*

And every time the trombone player swung his trombone he clunked one of the horn players round the head – *Clang!*

And every time the cymbal player crashed his cymbals together, the big bass drummer had his head caught right between them – *Crayangadanngg!* (No wonder he kept kicking the snare drummer up the you-know-what.)

So there was bound to be trouble.

AND THERE WAS.

The big bass drummer started shouting at the cymbal player. He couldn't turn round, because he was made of metal and he was only a clockwork model. But he could shout.

'Stop clashing your cymbals around my head, you stupid clanking clutterclod!'

The cymbal player was very surprised to hear himself called a stupid clanking clutterclod. He thought he was a very good cymbal player. He had no idea that the drummer's head was getting the worst of it. Anyhow, there was nothing he could do because he was only a clockwork model made of metal. He could only move as the toymaker had created him to.

'It's not my fault. I can't help it.' And to tell the truth the cymbal player did try to stop, but he couldn't. His arms were driven by the clockwork motor and he was like a robot. He had no control of his own.

But the big bass drummer was no longer paying any attention, because the snare drummer was shouting at *him*.

'You bumbling bang-bungler! Why do you keep kicking my backside? What's the matter with you? Ow! Stop it!'

And of course the bass drummer said, 'I can't help it. It's not my fault.' And to tell the truth he did try to stop, but he couldn't. His legs were driven by the clockwork motor and he was like a robot too. Every time his right leg shot out he kicked the snare drummer. Left, bumff! Left, bumff! And the pretty marching tune went ping, ping, ting-a-ding!

Meanwhile, the trombone player had swung his trombone against the horn player's head so many times that the poor man's head had come right off. It lay on the ground, where it was kicked about amongst the marching feet of all the other bandsmen. And while it rolled from one foot to another, it shouted angrily.

'Oi! You lot up there! Will you stop kicking me about? I'm not a football, you know! Look, I'm down here! Stop it, you kicking kipper-konks!'

But of course the soldiers couldn't do anything to stop their kicking. As long as the music went ping, ping, ting-a-ding, their feet went left, right, left, right. (Except for the bass drummer, who went left, bumff! Left, bumff! And the snare drummer, who went left, ow! Left, ow!)

The only bandsmen who thought all this was very funny were the flautists, the clarinettists and the trumpeters. They all thought it was hilarious, and they began spluttering with laughter into their instruments.

The fat conductor could not see what was happening behind him, because he was metal too, and couldn't turn his head. But he could hear all the noise and the shouting, and he wondered what on earth was happening. He began to shout back to the band, in a rather gruff voice, 'No talking in the ranks! No laughing down your trumpets! No sniggering amongst the flutes! Left! Right! Left! Oh! Whose head is that rolling about the floor? Who's lost their head? Is that one of the horns? Put your head back on at once. You're a disgrace to the regiment. I won't have you marching in my band with your head missing.'

Who knows how long this would have gone on for? Fortunately, something happened. Unfortunately, it wasn't very nice for the horn player because his head rolled under the right foot of one of the flute players and there it got stuck. It was well and truly wedged, so that every time the flautist's right leg came down it went *clunk!* right on the head of the horn player.

So now the bass drummer was going left, crayangadanngg! Left, crayangadanngg!

And the snare drummer was going left, bumff! Left, bumff!

And the horn player's head went clunk, ow! Clunk, ow!

And the pretty marching music went ping, ping, ting-a-ding.

The horn player's head was beginning to create problems. The flute player could no longer put down his right leg properly because the horn player's head was wedged beneath. This gradually made the flute player tip backwards. Every time he brought down his right foot, it hit the head, and because he could not bend his metal leg, his whole body was tipped backwards, further and further, until *splap!* He completely lost his balance and toppled back against one of the clarinettists.

'Watch yourself, you clumsy loon!' cried the clarinettist.

'Well, stop kicking my legs,' complained the flautist.

'I can't. You're leaning against me. I can't hold you up!'

'Now look what you've done!' yelled the flautist. 'My leg's come right off!'

'No talking in the ranks!' bellowed the fat conductor. 'Pick that leg up. I won't have any legs left lying around. You lot are a disgrace.'

'It's all right for you,' shouted the angry clarinettist. 'You're up at the front. You're all right.'

'Just keep going,' ordered the fat conductor. 'We've a job to do. Left, right, left, right.'

Then the clarinettist fell over, unable to support the flute player any longer. The horn player's head was no longer wedged beneath the flute player's foot and so that began to roll around the floor again.

It rolled beneath the fat conductor. He tripped, lost his balance and somehow managed to perform a complete twist-around, so that he was now facing his own marching band, while he marched backwards. The fat conductor was just in time to see the clarinettist topple back against the trumpeter, whose metal body broke in half. The top part of the trumpeter's body wobbled for a few seconds and then crashed to the floor.

'Oh dear,' said the trumpeter, before a horn player's foot crashed into his chest and got stuck. The foot was unable to carry on marching, and the cogs of the clockwork engine began to grate and grind.

'Keep on marching!' cried the fat conductor sternly, still stepping backwards. He was so horrified by what was happening to his beautiful band that he seemed to lose control of his heavy mace. All at once it went spinning up into the air. Sixteen pairs of eyes followed it as it went whirling upwards. Then down it came, spinning, spinning, spinning, as the marching band passed beneath, until flubba-dubba-THUDDD! It fell right in their midst. Both the trombone players lost their trombones (and their arms). One fell forward and the other fell backwards.

So now the fat conductor was going left, right, left, right, but backwards.

The flautist was going left, –, left, –, because his right leg was missing.

The bass drummer was going left, crayangadanngg! Left, crayangadanngg!

And the snare drummer was going left, bumff! Left, bumff!

And the horn player's head went clunk, ow! Clunk, ow!

The trombonists' legs went left, right, left, right, but the tops of their bodies were missing.

And by this time the pretty marching tune was not so pretty and it was beginning to go ping, plink, dung, ding, splap, klunk!

It got slower and slower as the clockwork wound down. The marching band became a weary procession, and at last they stopped.

The toymaker noted the silence from the front window of his shop. He left his bench and went off to wind up the wonderful carousel once more.

'What has happened here? Oh my, oh my!' The toymaker gazed dumbfounded at his creation and shook his head. 'I take my eyes off you for a few minutes and look what happens. What are we to do?'

He gathered up the marching band and took it back to his work table. He laboured night and day to put the music box to rights. It was an extraordinary piece of workmanship. The fat conductor held his long mace once more, while his little legs marched beneath his big fat belly, left, right, left, right!

Behind the conductor came the fifteen musicians. There were the two flautists, then the two clarinettists. They were followed by a pair of trumpeters, two horn players, two trombonists, two snare drummers, a brace of big bass drummers and a cymbal player .

The little carousel was wound up with a metal key and off they went, while the music box slowly unwound, tinkling its pretty marching tune once again. Round and round went the soldiers with their legs bravely snapping out, left, right, left, right.

The toymaker was delighted. He took the carousel back to the shop window, so that the passing world would see just what fine toys he could make. The conductor lifted his mace, round and round went the soldiers, left, right, left, right, and the pretty marching tune went ping, ping, ting-a-ding!

But, what the toymaker could not see was that the fat conductor's mace was working loose. It was gradually slipping through his hand. Sooner or later it would fall to the ground, and then . . .

ALL THE FUN

by Paul Cookson
illustrated by Nicholas Allan

Smell the smells and see the sights
Candyfloss and such delights
Taste the tastes and bite the bites
Here, there and everywhere
Fun-filled, noisy, neon nights
Fluorescent flashing lights
Waltzers waltzing left and right
Thrills and spills fill the air
Helter-skelter ghost-train frights
Ever faster speed excites
Loop-the-loop from dizzy heights
Flying round where eagles dare
Stomachs churning, turning tight
Faces gurning, burning bright
Rides that turn the knuckles white
All the fun ... all the fun ... all the fun of the faaaaaaaiiiiiiiii

BULLY-GOAT GRUFF

by **Chris Powling**
illustrated by **Chris Riddell**

*Some years ago, when my own children were very
small, we visited a fairground in southern France. And
there, right in the middle, was one of the most
beautiful carousels I've ever seen. It had the usual
horses and cockerels and ostriches, of course, all
moving up and down and round and round to that
wonderful carousel music.*

*We couldn't resist a ride, naturally. And, quite by
chance, I found myself sitting on a billy goat – except
it was a lot bigger and fiercer-looking than any billy
goat I'd come across before. When CAROUSEL asked
me for a story, preferably with a carousel connection,
to celebrate the twenty-fifth anniversary of the
magazine, I suddenly remembered that ride. Also, I
remembered that billy goat . . .*

Some stories seem to stick in your memory. You can't
shake them out of your head, however long they've
been there. For instance, do you remember the tale of
a certain Troll and three young billy goats? Here's a
detail or two to remind you:

A fast-flowing river . . .

A rickety, trip-trap bridge . . .

A flower-filled meadow on the other side all buzz-buzz-buzzing with honeybees . . .

Yes, it's the story of the three Billy-Goats Gruff. And it begins with Little Billy-Goat Gruff clip-clopping across the rickety, trip-trap bridge where the Troll lived.

But he didn't get very far.

Suddenly, he was nose to nose with the old Troll himself. 'You're just what I fancy for supper, kiddo!' he roared. 'I'll gobble up every bit of you – your horns, your hooves and all the hairs on your chinny-chin-chin!'

'Who, me, Mr Troll?' squeaked Little Billy-Goat Gruff. 'But I'm so small and skinny. Why not wait for my brother? He's much bigger than I am and he'll be here any minute.'

'Sounds good to me,' the old Troll slobbered.

And he let the billy goat pass.

This was his first mistake.

Middle Billy-Goat Gruff turned out to be just as clever. 'You shouldn't bother with me, Mr Troll,' he bleated. 'My brother's just coming and *his* horns and hooves are gigantic compared with mine. So are the hairs on his chinny-chin-chin, as it happens. Why spoil your appetite on a middle-sized billy goat?'

'Fair enough,' said the Troll, smacking his lips.

So he let the second goat pass as well.

This was his second mistake.

Soon afterwards, Big Billy-Goat Gruff arrived. Now, he was horrendously big – a hoofy, horny, heavyweight goat with a chinny-chin-chin so broad and bristly it looked like the fender on an old-fashioned steam train. Of course, a sensible Troll would have given up there and then. Not this one, though. Somehow, he still fancied his chances.

And this was his third and final mistake.

CRASH!

SPLASH!

GLUG-GLUG-GLUG!

Oh dear . . . goodbye, Mr Troll.

Fuming and foaming, the ugly old villain was swept away without the smallest bite of billy goat.

From that moment on, the bridge, the river and the flower-filled meadow on the other side all buzz-buzz-buzzing with honeybees became an utterly troll-free zone. That's why everyone who knows the story thinks that the three Billy-Goats Gruff lived happily ever after.

But they didn't.

In fact, their troubles had just begun.

The problem with winning so easily, you see, is that it can lead to showing off. And that's what happened to Big Billy-Goat Gruff. Soon he was swanking about like a superstar. He'd even written a song for himself:

I'M ROUGH AND I'M TOUGH!
I'M BULLY-GOAT GRUFF –

THE BIGGEST AND BEST OF THE THREE!
I BET I CAN BUTT YOU
(OR MAYBE I'LL EAT YOU)
YOU'D BETTER NOT MESS WITH ME!

His brothers could hardly believe it.

'*Bully*-Goat Gruff?' said Little Billy-Goat Gruff in dismay. 'Does that mean he's proud of being so hard and hefty?'

'I'm afraid so,' sighed Middle Billy-Goat Gruff. 'Now he's seen off the Troll, he wants to keep that flower-filled meadow all to himself. He won't even share it with us – his very own brothers. Every time we go near the trip-trap bridge, he threatens to duff us up.'

'Bruv, he threatens to duff up *everybody*. He says he couldn't care less who they are! Hey, look who's coming now – that's the local vicar, isn't it?'

The billy goats stared in horror.

For there was the vicar on her afternoon stroll.

Her cassock billowed in the breeze. Her face wore a gentle smile. Her hands were pressed together as if she were praying. Why, she looked as sweet and saintly as a figure in a stained-glass window. 'Just listen to the buzz-buzz-buzzing of those honeybees!' she cried. 'That flower-filled meadow is just the place for me to write my Sunday sermon. But how do I cross the river? Oh, bless! This is exactly what I need – a handy trip-trap bridge!'

'Don't do it!' baa'd the billy goats, wildly. 'Please don't do it, vicar! It's much too risky!'

But she was already on the bridge.

TRIPPETY-TRAP! TRIPPETY-TRAP! TRIPPETY-TRAP!

CRASH!

SPLASH!

GLUG-GLUG-GLUG!

At least the nastiness was over in an instant.

Well, maybe not quite an instant. As the poor, bedraggled vicar pulled herself soggily on to the riverbank, Bully-Goat Gruff was already singing his song:

'I'M ROUGH AND I'M TOUGH!
I'M BULLY-GOAT GRUFF –
THE BIGGEST AND BEST OF THE THREE!
I BET I CAN BUTT YOU
(OR MAYBE I'LL EAT YOU)
YOU'D BETTER NOT MESS WITH ME!'

The vicar gazed at him in sorrow.

She was much too upset to reply.

'He's *awful*!' Little Billy-Goat Gruff groaned.

'But he's still our brother,' said Middle Billy-Goat Gruff. 'There must be *something* we can do to cure him.'

And maybe he was right.

But neither of them had a clue what it was.

*

Next day, things grew even worse. Towards the end of the morning, when the sun was high in the sky, the two young billy goats were woken from their midday sleep. 'Who's that coming this way?' asked Little Billy-Goat Gruff in alarm.

'It's a teacher,' gasped Middle Billy-Goat Gruff. 'And she's leading a class of schoolchildren!'

They were lovely-looking children too.

So was their teacher. She had golden hair, bright blue eyes and a voice that was warm and friendly. 'Children, just listen to that wonderful buzz-buzz-buzzing,' she laughed. 'Those are honeybees gathering pollen – I've never heard them so loud! Let's have our picnic over there. It's the perfect spot for our Nature Study.'

'No! No!' squealed Little Billy-Goat Gruff.

'Go back to school!' shrieked his brother.

'Miss! Miss!' called one of the children. 'Why are those two billy goats making such a noise?'

'I expect they're hot, dear,' answered the teacher. 'And I'm not surprised, either, on a sunny day like this. Once we've reached that flower-filled meadow, we'll find somewhere shady to sit. Now, this bridge is a bit rickety, I'm afraid, so please be careful.'

Already she was leading them across.

About halfway across to be exact. Suddenly, the way was blocked by Bully-Goat Gruff, tossing his horns and scraping his hooves. 'Don't come any nearer, miss,' he snorted. 'Otherwise, a near-miss is just what you *won't* be – and I can't say fairer than that!'

'But that isn't fair at all!' said the lovely young teacher. 'This bridge is public property. Everyone is allowed to –'

TRIPPETY-TRAP! TRIPPETY-TRAP! TRIPPETY-TRAP!

CRASH!

SPLASH!

GLUG-GLUG-GLUG!

There were thirty-six crashes altogether – along with thirty-six splashes and thirty-six glug-glug-glugs – one for the lovely teacher and one each for her lovely children.

Even as they struggled out of the water, all shivery and sopping wet, they could see Bully-Goat Gruff wasn't in the least bit sorry. Instead, he was singing louder than ever:

'I'M ROUGH AND I'M TOUGH!
I'M BULLY-GOAT GRUFF –
THE BIGGEST AND BEST OF THE THREE!
I BET I CAN BUTT YOU
(OR MAYBE I'LL EAT YOU)
YOU'D BETTER NOT MESS WITH ME!'

His brothers had never felt more ashamed.

They'd never felt more helpless, either. 'Can't we tell him what a bully he's being?' asked Little Billy-Goat Gruff.

'He knows that already,' said his brother. 'That's why he calls himself Bully-Goat Gruff.'

'You mean he *likes* being a bully?'

'He loves it, bruv.'

'But that's terrible. Whenever he fancies a bit of crash, splash and glug-glug-glugging he simply duffs someone up! That can't be right, brother!'

Middle Billy-Goat Gruff shook his head, sadly. 'It isn't right,' he agreed. 'And it isn't fair, either: I agree with the teacher on that one. But what can we do to stop it – without being crash, splash and glug-glug-glugged ourselves, I mean?'

They both fell silent for a while.

What was there left to say, after all?

Bully-Goat Gruff was so hefty, hard and heavyweight, he could get away with pretty nearly anything. Was nobody strong enough to sort him out? 'Look, bruv!' exclaimed Little Billy-Goat Gruff. 'Someone else is coming now!'

'That's the village policeman, I think,' his brother gasped.

Quickly, they huddled together for comfort.

For the village policeman was very, very cross. He'd been sent to do his duty, anyone could see that. 'Hello-hello-hello,' he sniffed. 'Now what have we here? Could this be the cause of all the complaints I've been getting? Why, unless I'm very much mistaken, there's an obstruction up ahead. And the perpetrator of that obstruction is a farmyard personage at the other end of this bridge.'

He meant Bully-Goat Gruff, of course.

And he was already reaching for his notebook.

Bully-Goat Gruff wasn't impressed. 'Get back to

your cop shop, copper!' he shouted. 'Or you'll cop it good and proper!'

'I beg your pardon,' the policeman boomed. 'That's no way to talk to an Officer of the Law! Kindly –'

TRIPPETY-TRAP! TRIPPETY-TRAP! TRIPPETY-TRAP!

CRASH!

SPLASH!

GLUG-GLUG-GLUG!

The policeman didn't have a chance.

He clambered on to the towpath, dizzy from his ducking, dripping water from helmet to boots. As for his notebook, the fast-flowing river took care of that. So he couldn't even *report* what had happened when he got back to the police station.

Bully-Goat Gruff hadn't finished yet, though. He still had some singing to do:

'I'M ROUGH AND I'M TOUGH!
I'M BULLY-GOAT GRUFF –
THE BIGGEST AND BEST OF THE THREE!
I BET I CAN BUTT YOU
(OR MAYBE I'LL EAT YOU)
YOU'D BETTER NOT MESS WITH ME!'

His words sounded louder and bossier than ever.

Why, they almost smothered the buzz-buzz-buzzing of the honeybees in the flower-filled meadow across the river.

*

By now, his brothers were almost in despair. 'He's a monster, bruv,' sobbed Little Billy-Goat Gruff. 'We can't trust him to be nice to anyone.'

'Except someone as tough as he is, maybe,' said Middle Billy-Goat Gruff. 'He might take some notice, then. You know, I hate to admit it, but maybe biggest really is best after all!'

'No, it isn't,' came a voice from behind them.

The billy goats jumped in alarm.

Especially when they saw who it was.

'Yes, it's me again,' said the ugly old Troll. 'But there's no need to be panicky, kids. I won't harm the hairs on your chinny-chin-chins, I promise. Not any more I won't. I've already learned *my* lesson.'

'Have you?' said the billy goats, suspiciously.

The Troll rolled his eyes. 'When you're on the receiving end of a bit of crash, splash and glug-glug-glugging, it really changes the way you look at things. If you ask me, His Hoofiness up there on the bridge needs to find that out for himself.'

'How, though?' said Little Billy-Goat Gruff. 'He really is the biggest, isn't he? And that makes him the best as well.'

'Not necessarily, kid.'

'Sorry?'

The ugly old Troll tapped his nose. 'Biggest isn't always best,' he said. 'Sometimes it's much better to be small – that's if enough of you are working together.'

'Small?' said Middle Billy-Goat Gruff.

'And working together?' frowned his brother.

The billy goats looked at each other warily.

What on earth was the old Troll on about?

Then they saw where he was pointing – across the trip-trap bridge towards the flower-filled meadow across the river. He cupped a hand round one of his ears. 'Can you hear them?' he asked. 'They're ready when you are, you know.'

And he gave them a wink.

It was the oldest and craftiest wink they'd ever seen.

Was it really better to be small . . . provided enough of you are working together?

There was only one way to find out.

So the Troll took charge of the operation, personally. This time, it was Bully-Goat Gruff who was woken from his midday snooze. 'Who's that disturbing my beauty sleep?' he yawned. 'Another trespasser on my trip-trap bridge? I'll soon have them sorted!'

'Hello, brother . . .' said Little Billy-Goat Gruff.

That was all he had time for.

Bully-Goat Gruff was already singing his song:

'I'M ROUGH AND I'M TOUGH!
I'M BULLY-GOAT GRUFF –
THE BIGGEST AND BEST OF THE THREE!
I BET I CAN BUTT YOU
(OR MAYBE I'LL EAT YOU)
YOU'D BETTER NOT MESS WITH ME!'

'Eat me, brother?' exclaimed Little Billy-Goat Gruff in surprise. 'Right now, do you mean? When you're about to get a visit from the Queen and all her followers?'

'The Queen and all her followers?' blinked Bully-Goat Gruff. 'She's visiting *me*? She must have heard how strong and handsome I am! OK, squirt. You can cross the bridge if you like. Get lost in the daisies and buttercups.'

And he let his little brother pass.

This was his first mistake.

Middle Billy-Goat Gruff was next. 'Hello, brother . . .' he began.

'Hey, you're not a Royal!' snarled Bully-Goat Gruff. 'You're just another billy goat. Maybe you've forgotten how special I am:

I'M ROUGH AND I'M TOUGH!
I'M BULLY-GOAT GRUFF –
THE BIGGEST AND BEST OF THE THREE!
I BET I CAN BUTT YOU –'

'Butt me, brother?' said Middle Billy-Goat Gruff. 'When the Queen and all her followers are almost here?'

'Almost here?' gasped Bully-Goat Gruff. 'Already? OK, semi-squirt, chill out among the daisies and buttercups. I can't be bothered with the likes of you.'

And he let his middle-sized brother pass.

This was his second mistake.

Almost at once, the old Troll appeared on the scene.

'Er . . . good day, Mr Gruff,' he said.

Bully-Goat Gruff was furious. 'You again?' he hissed. 'Don't you remember what happened last time? Here's a reminder:

I'M ROUGH AND I'M TOUGH!
I'M BULLY-GOAT GRUFF –'

'Excuse me, Lord Gruff . . .' said the Troll.

'Lord Gruff?'

'Well, that's who you might be after you've met the Queen and all her followers. She's sent me ahead to announce her.'

'She's arrived, you mean?' exclaimed Bully-Goat Gruff. 'Well, whiz your butt into the meadow behind me, uglymug. I'd better practise a bit of bowing and scraping.'

And he let the Troll cross the bridge.

This was his third and last mistake.

Suddenly, from the flower-filled meadow behind him, he noticed a buzz-buzz-buzzing sound – a fat and honey-stuffed buzz-buzz-buzzing sound that was definitely getting louder. 'What's that?' he snorted. 'It can't be the Queen and all her followers, can it?'

But it was.

The whole swarm was coming closer . . .

Closer . . .

CLOSER . . .

and *CLOSER*.

Bully-Goat Gruff kicked up his hooves in fright. '*That*

kind of Queen?' he yelped. 'And *those* kind of followers?'

BUZZ-BUZZ! BUZZ-BUZZ! BUZZ-BUZZ!

Yes, sometimes it's good to be big, all right.

But often it's better to be small . . . provided there's a lot of you working together.

It would be cruel to describe in detail what the honeybees did to Bully-Goat Gruff. Let's just say they chased him backwards and forwards, hither and thither, this way and that, across every inch of the flower-filled meadow across the river. 'Stop it, Your Majesty!' he kept screaming. 'Please stop it!'

But there was only one way to escape.

The Queen made sure he took it, too.

TRIPPETY-TRAP! TRIPPETY-TRAP! TRIPPETY-TRAP!

CRASH!

SPLASH!

GLUG! GLUG! GLUG!

And that was the end of Bully-Goat Gruff.

Well . . . almost. He still hangs out in the flower-filled meadow, of course. These days, though, it's perfect for billy goats of *all* sizes. Also it's perfect for vicars, village policemen, schoolteachers and whole classes of lovely children doing their Nature Study. In fact, it's just about perfect for everyone – including trolls.

Suppose someone else takes a fancy to a bit of crash, splash and glug-glug-glugging, though?

Don't worry.

The Queen and all her followers keep a sharp lookout for anyone who's in danger of showing off. As they flit about in the bright summer sun, gathering honey to their hearts' content, you can hear them singing this song:

'WE BET WE CAN BUZZ YOU!
OR MAYBE WE'LL *STING* YOU –
YOU'D BETTER NOT MESS WITH A BEE!'

And, believe me, nobody does.

ALL THE GOLDEN HORSES

by Adèle Geras
illustrated by Shirley Hughes

'*I*'ve found three gingham patches, Aunt Pinny. All together in a bunch here.'

'Yes, I remember those. Pink and white, brown and white, and blue and white checks. My mother made me three new pinafores for my first holiday in the country.'

'Where did you go?' I asked.

'To stay with Jessie, my mother's second cousin. She owned a small cottage, just outside Oxford. I had been ill a great deal during the previous winter and spring, and my mother felt the country air would do me good. We went to stay for four weeks: the last two weeks of August and the first two weeks in September. I remember that because of the fair. St Giles' Fair in Oxford is always at the beginning of September.'

'Did you go? Do you like fairs? Did anything exciting happen?'

'I'll tell you all about it, shall I?' said Aunt Pinny.

'Yes, please,' I said. Aunt Pinny put her sewing down on the chest of drawers, and came to sit at the foot of the bed.

It's nothing to you, I know, to jump into an aeroplane and fly high as a cloud to the other side of the earth. Men have already walked on the moon and, I dare say, you too will be able to go there one day, although it's not a place that I would enjoy, I feel. When I was small, even a trip on the top deck of an omnibus was exciting, and when I was seven, I had never been on a train, never been pulled along behind a real steam engine. And I had never been to the country.

'It's not the proper country, Pinny,' my mother warned me. 'Oxford is a large town, and quite near. Cousin Jessie doesn't live on a farm, you know.'

Still, and in spite of all my mother's talk, I had a picture in my head of what the country was like: milkmaids in mob caps and farmers in knee breeches, small houses with roses growing over the doors, stiles, carthorses, shepherds coming down from the hills at sunset, wooden bridges curving over brooks. For a week before we left London, I packed and repacked my case. The three pinafores were ready, with frills running over the shoulders and round the hem. They had big, deep pockets. Perhaps Cousin Jessie would give me a wicker basket, and I could collect eggs from the henhouse for tea. Brown eggs. I could see it all.

'Cousin Jessie doesn't keep hens, dear,' said my mother when I asked her. That did not really worry me. The image of myself in a frilled, gingham pinafore with a basket of brown eggs over my arm was stronger than the truth.

We left from Paddington Station. The steam hissed from the engines and stung my nostrils and my eyes. Puffs of blue smoke rose into the iron and glass roof, the highest roof that I had ever seen. In our compartment we put our cases into a luggage rack that was like a fishing net on a wooden frame, and did not seem strong enough to take the weight of our baggage. All the way to Oxford I worried about it. I was sure it was going to break. When the train started, I listened to the metal clacking of the wheels, and the huffing of the steam. We could see the backs of houses from the window. They looked too small to belong to real people. Children in the little squares of back gardens waved at the train as it went by, and I waved back. Then we left London behind, and fields and green hedges and bushy trees slid past. I even saw real cows, although they too looked smaller than I had imagined. In the compartment there were yellowing photographs of buildings with tall towers, and two spotted brown mirrors. Just before we arrived in Oxford, the ladies looked into the mirrors, patted their hats and put down their veils, and the gentlemen lifted all the cases out of the nets, which had held firm, after all.

'I'll look out, dear, and see if I can see Jessie,' said my mother, and I looked out of the window too, even though I had never seen Cousin Jessie before. She would, I thought, be a comfortable-looking person in a bonnet, with a lace shawl around her shoulders, and an apron over her skirt. Her cheeks would be pink, of course, from the country air.

'There she is,' said my mother, and fluttered a handkerchief out of the window. I could see nobody on the platform like the picture-book farmer's wife I had imagined. I followed my mother to the barrier, and Cousin Jessie was waiting there. As I kissed her politely, I thought: *She's just like an ordinary London person*. She was not ordinary at all, however. She was the tallest lady I had ever seen, with sad eyes and cheeks as pale as paper, that felt papery when I kissed her. She wore a black hat and a black cotton dress, and her hands were bony in black lace gloves. I didn't think I liked her very much, except for her voice. When she spoke, I wished she would never stop. Her voice was like a lullaby.

We drove to the cottage in a pony and trap. I was a little upset to discover that they were borrowed from a neighbour for the occasion, but I felt I was in the country already, trotting in the sun through the wide, tree-studded streets of Oxford.

The cottage was a disappointment. It was one of a terrace of small, grey stone houses with front doors opening straight on to the road. There were no roses anywhere. There were no front gardens, just a row of brown-painted doors, one after the other. On the other side of the road was another row of houses, just the same, and at the end of the road I could see a patch of grass. There were two benches on the grass, and a duck pond with some ducks swimming around it, half-heartedly.

'That's the village green,' said Cousin Jessie. 'Over beyond the pond is the shop and the local inn, the Golden Lion.' She opened the cottage door, and we went down two steps into a shady room with a floor made out of big squares of butter-yellow stone. It was cool, and it took a little while for my eyes to grow used to the dim light after the glare outside. Cousin Jessie did not believe in a great deal of furniture. There was an upright piano against one wall, a rocking chair and two hard chairs with rush seats. In the fireplace stood a brown jar full of wild flowers whose names I did not know.

'I like these silvery ones,' I said, touching, the flat, almost transparent discs.

'Honesty they're called,' said Cousin Jessie.

The only other rooms downstairs were the kitchen and larder. A large, square table sat under the window. A black stove, a stone sink and a cupboard full of pots and pans and cups and saucers were the only other things in the room. I looked out of the window.

'There's a garden!' I said. 'May I go and see?'

'Yes, dear,' said my mother, and Cousin Jessie said: 'That little shed at the end of the garden path is the lavatory. You'll have your baths in the kitchen here, in that big tub.' She pointed to a tin bath I had not noticed before, on the floor of the larder.

The garden was a long strip of grass cut into two by

a flagstone path. All along the fence that divided Cousin Jessie's garden from the one next door, the sunflowers grew, a forest of giants, twice as tall as I was, with loose, golden petals, dark brown centres the size of plates and jungle-thick leaves. I did not know flowers could grow so tall. It didn't seem right. They were alive in a way that small flowers were not, nodding in the breeze, each one staring at me out of its single, furry eye. I wished Cousin Jessie grew roses, like everyone else. I hurried indoors again.

My mother and I were to share a room. On that first night, I went to bed as the light was fading, and lay for a long time staring at the white walls and the unfamiliar shapes of chair and cupboard. A pale ribbon of light from the lamp downstairs crept under the door and made shadows I didn't like. I looked out of the window. The sunflowers were asleep, petals hanging down and stems bending over. I jumped back into bed and buried my face in the pillow.

At breakfast Cousin Jessie said, 'I hope you won't be bored, Pinny. There's not a great deal to do here.'

'Are there no children?' I asked.

'Yes, I suppose so,' Cousin Jessie frowned. 'But I don't know them very well. They seem loud and boisterous, and they are never very . . .' Her voice faded away.

'Very what?'

'Well, very friendly. They seem, I know it's ridiculous, but they seem . . . nervous of me.'

I looked at Cousin Jessie and understood exactly how the unknown children must feel. She was too tall, and too thin and too pale. I was, I think, a little frightened of her myself. My mother said, 'Pinny will go to the shop for you, Jessie. Won't you, dear?'

'Oh yes.' I was pleased. I liked shopping. 'May I go alone?'

'Yes, it's only just across the green,' said Cousin Jessie. 'I shall give you a list, some money and the basket.'

I walked across the green with a basket over my arm, and pretended it was full of eggs. A boy and a girl, both bigger than me, were sitting beside the duck pond, tearing blades of grass in half. They looked at me and giggled. The boy did have knee-breeches on, but the girl was not a milkmaid. She was wearing a pinafore over her dress, just like me, and her long hair blew about in the sunshine. I could feel them looking at my back, and my plaits seemed tight and prim to me. Their laughter followed me as I walked round the pond.

The shop smelled of bacon, candles, tea, paper and glue. One side of it was a post office, fenced off behind wire mesh. The food part of the shop was on the other side. 'Can I help you, miss?' The lady at the counter was smiling from behind a mountain of butter.

'Yes, please,' I said, and I told her what I needed. As she padded round the shop finding eggs and tea, slicing bacon, scooping balls of butter from the shining yellow slopes on the counter, she talked. She asked questions too, and answered them herself.

'You're the London child, of course you are. Skinny and pale. This butter'll soon see the roses back in your cheeks. Jessie Fraser is some kind of relation, isn't that the truth of it? A cousin, that's it. Just what she needs, a bit of company. Been alone too long, that's what's wrong. Shut up inside herself. Won't share her troubles. Nothing else wrong at all, though I do know what they say – no more music now, not like in the old days. Not since he died. She was quite happy before, mind, but not since he died. Garden gone to rack and ruin. Nothing but those sunflowers. Too big, they are. Not natural. Young person'll be very good for her.' The door of the shop opened and the two children from the duck pond came in and sat down on sacks of flour beside the counter. They looked at me.

'What's your name?' said the boy.

'Pinny.'

'That's stupid,' he said, and they started laughing and clutching each other, and pointing at me. The lady behind the counter hit them gently on the head with a wooden spoon.

'Now, Miles, now, Kate, manners. This is Mrs Fraser's cousin from London. Yokels, she'll think you are. Mind you behave now.' The boy leaped off the flour sack and held out his hand.

'Sorry,' he said, 'we didn't know you were all the way from London. I'm Miles and this is Kate, my sister. She's a bit silly sometimes.' He hopped about on one foot, rubbing his other shin where Kate had just kicked him.

'Hurry up and finish in here, and then come and tell us all about London,' said Kate. 'We'll wait for you by the duck pond. Don't be long.'

I told them all about London. They listened with their mouths hanging open. They had never been further than Oxford. Then they told me about the village and the countryside.

'I must go now,' I said at last. 'It's nearly lunchtime.'

'Back you go then, to the Haunted House. Beware,' said Miles.

'What Haunted House?' My voice wobbled a little.

'Mrs Fraser's. It's haunted. By her husband. He died ages ago, but he RETURNS.'

'I didn't see him last night,' I muttered.

'Well, it stands to reason you wouldn't see him,' said Kate. 'You'll hear him. He used to play the piano, and some nights he comes back and plays again: ghostly, ghastly music. You listen tonight.' She groaned, and Miles rattled imaginary chains. Then they began to giggle and Kate chewed a strand of her own hair.

'I don't believe you, so there,' I said. 'And I'm going. Goodbye.'

They were still laughing. As I walked away, Kate shouted after me: 'Come tomorrow and we'll climb the big elm.'

That night, I stayed awake as long as I could, and heard nothing. We climbed the elm the next day, and Miles and Kate took me to their house for tea. It was the last cottage on Cousin Jessie's side of the road. It seemed smaller than Cousin Jessie's. Mrs Armitage, the children's mother, and their thick-set father who smoked a pipe, Miles and Kate with their wide smiles and flying hair filled the rooms with their movement and talk. We ate bread out of the oven and home-made jam. Kate said, 'No music yet?'

'You wait,' said Miles. 'You wait and see.'

'I don't believe it,' I said.

'Well, you've got to admit she's odd, your cousin,' said Kate.

'Enough of that, girl,' said Mrs Armitage, lifting the cosy from the brown teapot. 'She's a widow. She misses her husband. Nothing odd about that. It's all nonsense, this music lark; I've told you often enough. Now, hold your tongues, both of you, or you'll be scaring young Pinny.'

Miles and Kate looked serious. Miles said quietly: 'It's true, Mother. We've heard it, haven't we, Kate?'

Kate put down her teacup and looked at her mother. 'Yes, we have. It's the truth, Mother.'

Mrs Armitage put the cosy back on to the teapot. 'Change the subject, children,' she said, and looked strangely at them. 'You'll all be having nightmares tonight.'

That night, I could not sleep. My mother lay in the bed next to mine, and it made me feel happier to see the shape of her in the moonlight. I strained my ears, hearing creaks and groans in the furniture that I had never heard before. After a long time, I began to drift into sleep. At first I thought I was dreaming, but I woke up and sat upright in bed, and I could still hear it. Music. Piano music, played very softly, picked out with one finger. I listened to the tune, a thin, pretty waltz, and then I could bear it no longer. I shook my mother.

'Mama, can you hear it? The music? They were right. It's a ghost.'

'What? What are you doing, Pinny? Have you had a bad dream?' My mother was awake in a moment, hugging me. I told her about the ghost of Cousin Jessie's husband.

Then I said: 'Listen, you'll hear it.' There was nothing in the silence except the night noises of the house.

'Pinny, you must go to sleep. Believe me, it was a dream,' said my mother.

'It wasn't a dream. It was the ghost of Mr Fraser.'

'Don't be a little goose. Clarence was a very gifted pianist. You said the music you heard was picked out with one finger. Surely a musical ghost could manage a few chords?'

I laughed at that and closed my eyes at last, with my mother holding my hand across the space between the beds.

Miles and Kate were thrilled when I told them the next morning that I really had heard the music.

They tried to persuade me to go down to the front room if I heard it again, to see if I could catch a glimpse of the ghost.

'Never,' I said. 'I'd never do that. I'd die of fright.'

'Cowardy custard,' Kate said.

'Shut up, Kate,' said Miles. 'You know you'd never dare either.'

'Neither would you, so there,' said Kate, and for a while they rolled around in the grass, pushing handfuls of it into each other's mouths, and laughing and laughing.

'Stop! Pax!' Miles yelled. 'You're right, I wouldn't dare either. But, Pinny, you're to listen again, and report anything you hear or see. It would be interesting to know if your cousin Jessie hears it.'

I heard the music again that night. Again, the waltz was played falteringly three times, and after that I only heard the silence. In the morning, I went downstairs early and found Cousin Jessie pushing some sheet music into the piano stool. She seemed surprised to see me.

'Goodness, Pinny, you're up very early. I was just tidying up.' She laughed, although she had not said anything funny.

'Do you play the piano?' I asked.

'Oh no, no, I don't. Not at all.' Cousin Jessie looked away. 'Clarence, my late husband, used to play a great deal, but now the piano is . . .' she paused, '. . . still.'

I thought of Miles and Kate and said, 'Do you ever hear the piano in the middle of the night?'

Again Cousin Jessie laughed, although this time I had not said anything funny.

'The piano? In the night? You must have been dreaming. Who would play the piano now? I must make the breakfast.'

That afternoon, Miles, Kate and I went walking in the fields.

'She must hear it,' said Miles.

'Maybe she's asleep,' said Kate.

We ran races to the far hedge, and forgot about the music in the clear light.

I did not hear the waltz in the night after that day. A few days later it was difficult to believe that I had ever heard it. Miles and Kate hardly mentioned it any more. We were busy through the long, sunshiny days: playing in the fields around the village, fishing in the brooks with nets on the end of long rods, paddling with our socks off and our clothes rolled up, running, climbing and lying in the high grass looking up and up at the towering green spears.

Then we began to look forward to the fair. St Giles' Fair, said Miles and Kate, was the most splendid, exciting, glorious fair in the whole world, and we were going to it in three days, in two days, in one more day.

The day came. The three of us travelled to the fair with my mother and Cousin Jessie in the pony and trap. We were still quite far away when we heard the sound of the steam organs. When we arrived, I was overwhelmed. The whole street was full of tents and booths. The music of the roundabouts drowned the shouts of children. The helter-skelter slide and the toffee apples, the Wild Man of Borneo, the Amazing Reptile Pit, the Incredible Madame Zara: Your Fortune Told for One Penny – we did not know where to go first. Even Cousin Jessie looked happy. She had pinned a cluster of artificial cherries to the brim of her black hat. Miles and Kate and I tried everything. Kate won a prize for shooting: a little goldfish in a bowl. Madame Zara told Miles he would travel far away, which pleased him. I ate three toffee apples and wasted most of my pennies trying to throw a hoop around a brush and comb set which looked as though it were made of silver.

Miles said suddenly: 'We haven't been on that,' and pointed towards a roundabout, half-hidden behind the helter-skelter.

'Look,' said Kate. 'Isn't it the most wonderful one?' We all went up to it and stood and stared. There were curly, gilded bits all around the top. The horses were frozen in a gallop, snorting through pink-flared nostrils rimmed with gold. Their manes were the colour of fire and carved into wooden dancing flames.

A voice from the heart of the roundabout shouted, 'Roll up, roll up! All the golden horses are ready for a ride. All the golden horses. Take your seats, boys and girls. All the golden horses are riding off in two minutes. Roll up, roll up for the golden horses!'

The music started slowly at first, then became faster and faster, mechanical music, galloping up and down music. I did not notice it at first. I clung to the scarlet pole in the middle of my horse's back. I could see Kate's hair floating out behind her, and I heard Miles shouting something. It was only when the music slowed down at the end of the ride, and I could see my mother and Cousin Jessie standing in the crowd, that I recognized the tune. It was the very same tune that the ghost had played, although it sounded rich and jangling coming from the roundabout. We dismounted. The golden horses set off again, and we watched them.

I whispered to Miles and Kate: 'That's the tune. That's what the ghost plays.'

Miles said: 'We must ask Cousin Jessie about it. I'm sure she knows something. Look at her.' Cousin Jessie was gazing at the whirling horses and swaying slightly in time to the music.

'Do you know the name of this tune?' I said.

'It's called "The Roundabout Waltz",' said Cousin Jessie. 'Clarence used to play it. It has words too.'

'Please tell us,' we said. 'We'd love to hear the words.'

Cousin Jessie began to sing softly:

'Ride with me tonight on a swift, golden horse
Whose black hooves will never touch ground.
Golden horses will carry you all round the stars,
As the roundabout music goes round.'

'You've got a beautiful voice, Mrs Jessie,' said Kate, and Miles added: 'I never knew you could sing like that.'

'I don't sing very much these days,' said Cousin Jessie.

'That's a great pity,' said my mother. 'You should sing.'

We went home in the starlight. The music of the fair went round and round and faded away behind us. No one said anything. Then Cousin Jessie, who was holding the reins, said: 'I have tried. Really I have. To sing, I mean. But I can't play, and it sounds so thin without the piano. Sometimes, just to remember what it was like, I take out the sheet music and try the tune with one finger. It doesn't sound as it used to. I generally play at night, because I don't want anyone to hear . . .' Cousin Jessie smiled, 'especially not Clarence, wherever his ghost may be.' She looked at me. 'I'm sorry I woke you up, Pinny. I should've confessed at once, shouldn't I, instead of pretending it never happened?'

Miles, Kate and I began to laugh. Cousin Jessie looked a little shocked. I said: 'I'm sorry, Cousin Jessie, we're not laughing at you, only at ourselves.'

We told her all about the ghost, and then she laughed too, and so did my mother. We must have woken a good many people in the village as we rode up to our door.

Cousin Jessie changed after that night. My mother

played the piano a little, and the next afternoon Miles and Kate came to tea and Cousin Jessie sang us 'The Roundabout Waltz'. Then we all sang together, every tune we could remember. We had an iced cake that Cousin Jessie had made herself that morning. She was wearing a mauve dress, instead of a black one, and she had cut three sunflowers and placed them in a vase on the kitchen table.

Maybe I hadn't seen them properly in the garden. Perhaps they looked different seen from underneath. They seemed more friendly on the kitchen table: sunnier and more gentle. Their yellow petals shone in the light, and made it brighter. 'They're very pretty, really, aren't they, Cousin Jessie?' I said.

'They can be,' said Cousin Jessie, 'in the proper place. The thing is, they're so tall no one ever looks them in the eye, if you see what I mean.'

Our time in the country went very quickly after that. On the morning we left, Miles and Kate came with me to borrow the pony and trap that would take us to the station in Oxford.

'Will you tell us your address in London?' Kate asked. 'If we ever go there, we'll come and see you.' She took a chewed-up pencil stub and a dirty sheet of paper from her pinafore pocket, and I wrote down my address.

'We could write letters to one another,' said Miles.

'Oh yes. Yes, we will,' I said. Kate took out another sheet of paper and wrote their address down for me.

'We've got a present for you,' they said. 'It's at home.' We stopped at their house on the way to Cousin Jessie's, and Kate presented me with a bunch of wilting flowers. Miles gave me half of his nail collection: five fine, straight, silvery nails with grooves curling round the bottom in a spiral, and neat, flat heads.

Miles and Kate waved to us as we rode off. They went on waving, and so did I, until the pony and trap went over the bridge and turned towards Oxford.

'Did you ever see them again? Did you write to each other?' I asked.

'We wrote a few letters, but gradually the time between the letters grew longer, and the letters themselves shorter until there were no letters left. I never saw Miles and Kate again and, to tell you the truth, I'd half-forgotten them after a year or two. I remembered enough about the fun we'd had, though, to sew three patches into the quilt when I outgrew my pinafores. Cousin Jessie sold the cottage and became a choir mistress in Ely, and it was only when I was already grown up that I happened to be in Oxford again and visited the village. Mr and Mrs Armitage were still there, very old and stiff. They hardly remembered who I was. Miles was in the Merchant Navy and Kate was a teacher in Scotland. I remember them both very clearly now that I'm older and, of course, I have the patchwork to remind me.'

Aunt Pinny took her sewing from the chest of drawers, and kissed me goodnight.

MELANIE BELL

by Jack Ousbey

illustrated by Harry Horse

Melanie Bell, Melanie Bell,
Why are you going on the carousel?
'To break a world record,' she replied,
'For the longest time on a fairground ride.
I've a flask of tea, some cheese, some bread,
And I'll be back home tomorrow,' she said.

But tomorrow came, and where was Mel?
She was still going round on the carousel.
Round and round like a spinning top
Until poor Melanie cried out, 'Stop!
I've finished my tea and eaten my bread,
The cheese is stale and I'm tired,' she said.

But round and round went the carousel
And round and round went Melanie Bell.
'I've broken the record,' Melanie cried.
'I'm sorry,' the man in charge replied.
'Just what it is I cannot tell,
But something's gone wrong with the carousel.'

Let us stand and pray for Melanie Bell,
Who can't escape from the carousel.
Her attempt on the record was most unsound.
Now she'll just go round and round and round and round and round and round and round and round and round and round and round and round and round and

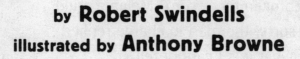

CAROUSEL

by **Robert Swindells**
illustrated by **Anthony Browne**

There was once a couple called Pete and Patricia who had everything they wanted except a baby. They lived in a pretty cottage with a beautiful garden in a peaceful village. They had top jobs, fast cars and digital TV. Four times a year they'd pack designer clothes into matching leather suitcases and jet off to somewhere romantic such as Bali, Tangier or Trinidad. Everybody envied them and thought they were blissfully happy but they were not, because everywhere they looked there were babies. In prams and slings and car-seats, wriggling in mothers' arms or riding on daddies' shoulders, the world seemed full of crowing, roly-poly babies who didn't belong to Pete and Patricia.

'It's not fair,' said Patricia. 'With our money we could give a baby everything. Why do poor people get a houseful of babies without even trying, when we can't manage *one*?'

Pete shook his head. 'We must be patient, Patricia: it'll be our turn eventually, you'll see.'

'I've *been* patient,' grumbled Patricia, 'but it's never our turn. I don't think it ever will be.'

But Patricia was wrong.

One cold winter's day, she and Pete were standing beside the baggage carousel at the airport, waiting for their luggage to appear. They'd flown in from Barbados looking tanned and fit, but long-haul flights are exhausting and the couple couldn't wait to get home for a pot of good English tea and a long sleep. Their plane had been full so there was quite a scrum round the carousel, which hummed and clunked as it trundled a procession of bags and parcels past the tired travellers. Now and then somebody would lunge, swing a bag off the moving belt on to a trolley and hurry away, glad to be clear of the throng. Little by little the crowd thinned, till the carousel was empty and only Pete and Patricia were left.

'What's happening?' growled Pete, his eyes fixed on the hatch that the moving belt emerged from. 'Where are *our* bags?'

Patricia sighed. 'They've probably loaded them on to a plane by mistake: they'll be halfway to Australia by now.'

'No, here they come at last,' cried Pete, as an object pushed through the curtain of hanging ribbons which covered the hatch. It was a black leather holdall, but it wasn't theirs. They watched it approach, wondering whose it could be, since everybody had gone. 'Perhaps it belongs to the Captain,' murmured Patricia. 'He's taken ours and left his.'

Pete was about to reply when an odd thing happened. As the bag trundled past, the couple heard a baby's cry. It wasn't very loud but it was definitely a baby. They glanced round the empty baggage hall, then looked at each other. 'Where . . .?' began Pete.

'*The holdall!*' squealed Patricia. 'There's a baby in the holdall!'

It was past them now, heading for the exit hatch. Pete started after it but Patricia caught his sleeve. 'Wait here,' she said, 'it'll come round again.'

It did, and this time they were ready. Pete lifted it off the belt and put it gently on the floor. Patricia watched as he opened the zip. They'd forgotten all about their luggage. The zip ran smoothly along its track and there, on a blanket in the bottom of the holdall lay a tiny, blue-eyed baby. It had no clothes on so the couple could see at once it was a little girl. 'Oh, Pete!' gasped Patricia. 'Just look at her: what a *sweetie.*' She lifted the child out of the bag. 'I know: we'll call her *Carousel*, because . . .'

'Hey, just a *minute*, Patricia.' Pete took hold of her elbow, gently. 'We won't call her *anything*, sweetheart. We can't; she's not ours.'

'Whose *is* she then?' Patricia stood, cradling the baby in her arms, looking round the deserted hall. 'There's nobody here. Nobody's looking for her. What would you do: pop her back in the bag, plonk it on the belt, watch it vanish through the hatch?' She shook her head. 'I'm not giving up this baby: not for *anything*. I've waited too long.'

Pete was about to protest when she cried, 'Look, Pete: here come the cases. Grab them and let's go before anything else happens.'

He argued, saying they must leave the baby with the airport staff, but Patricia was adamant. He'd never seen her so determined, nor so happy. He found himself hurrying after her with the trolley as she took the green track through Customs with the baby in her arms, nothing to declare.

Before he knew it, he was unlocking the car, loading the boot and settling Patricia in the back seat with the baby in its blanket on her lap. As he slipped into the driver's seat and fitted the key into the ignition, she smiled dreamily and said, 'Tomorrow we must see about having a child seat fitted.'

For the next few days, Pete was on tenterhooks, listening for the knock on the door which was bound to come. It didn't. Every morning he scanned his newspaper, but there was no story about a missing baby. Patricia, powdering Carousel's bottom, smiled. 'You're worrying about nothing, Pete: nobody's looking for this baby because nobody lost her. She's a *magic* baby.'

Pete didn't believe in magic, but as the days stretched out into weeks he stopped listening for knocks and looking for stories. Patricia was totally besotted with Carousel, and he was growing more fond of her himself. There was a child seat now, and a cot and a pram and three big drawers filled with designer babywear. None of the neighbours seemed to think it strange that the Cockcrofts suddenly had this baby: nobody asked questions or gave them funny looks. In fact, they'd bend over the pram and tickle Carousel's cheek and say she was the spitting image of Patricia.

Time passed. Carousel learned to crawl, then to walk. She wasn't really the spitting image of Patricia: she was far too pretty for that. She was easily the best-looking toddler in the neighbourhood. Patricia took to fussing with the child's hair, dressing her up like a fashion model and parading her up and down the road for people to admire. If Carousel overbalanced and sat down with a bump as toddlers do, Patricia would sweep her up and carry her into the house, tutting about the mess she'd made of her clothes. The poor child would be stripped, scrubbed and bundled into a new outfit before she'd had time to draw breath. Then Patricia would give her hair a fierce brushing, tugging the bristles through the infant's curls as if she were currying a horse. Carousel was the prettiest child in the neighbourhood, but she was not the happiest.

'Patricia,' said Pete one day, when he'd watched his partner smoothing blue stuff on the child's eyelids with her little finger and tinting her mouth with just the tiniest hint of lipstick, 'babies don't need that stuff, they're pretty in themselves. And why all this designer kit, when Carousel would be perfectly content in a pair of old dungarees, rolling about in the dirt and putting worms in her mouth?'

Patricia shuddered. 'I waited years for this baby, Pete. Years and years, and all I dreamed about was washing and powdering and dressing and grooming and keeping nice. There was no dirt in my dream, and no worms.'

Pete shook his head. 'Carousel isn't *you*, Patricia: she's herself. I think maybe she just wants to get mussed-up and sticky like other kids. You know: grazed knees, clots of dried pudding in her hair, all that.'

Patricia sighed. 'You obviously don't know the first thing about little girls, Pete. They *love* dressing up, wearing lipstick, having hair like Mummy's. Perhaps you should stick to what you know and leave Carousel to me.'

One warm afternoon when Pete was out at work and Carousel was sitting very still on a garden chair so as not to crease her expensive jeans, Patricia found a piece in her magazine about a competition. 'Hey, Caro,' she chirped, 'listen to this.' She knew Carousel wasn't old enough really to understand the piece, but she didn't believe in talking down to children so she read it out. It seemed there was to be a competition to find the prettiest little girl in the land. All you had to do was send in a snapshot of your child, and a panel of experts would look at all the photographs and decide which was the prettiest. The winner would get one thousand pounds *and* the chance to become a child model.

'Don't want to be a model,' sulked Carousel, listening to the neighbours' children laughing and shouting in the lane. 'I want to go play.' She didn't know what a model was, but if Patricia was excited it was bound to involve sitting still and wearing stiff new clothes.

Patricia smiled. 'Don't be silly, Carousel: *every* little girl wants to be a model. Now come inside and get into that new frock while Mummy finds a photographer in Yellow Pages.'

So off they drove to the photographer's studio. 'My, what a *gorgeous* frock,' gushed the photographer, and he made Carousel pose against various silly backgrounds while he took shots of her. It was hot in the studio. Carousel got fed up. 'Smile,' ordered the photographer, 'you're having your picture taken, not all your teeth out.' Carousel smiled till her face ached.

The prints would be ready in a week. Patricia could hardly wait. Carousel didn't care. In fact, she forgot all about it, as three-year-olds do.

When they came, the prints were sensational. Patricia wished she could put them in the Post Office window where all the neighbours would see them and be jealous. She chose the best one and posted it off to the competition. Pete framed one of the others and hung it in the living room. Carousel thought she looked like somebody's doll.

Weeks passed, then a letter came. Patricia opened it and squealed. 'I've *won*! Pete, I've won the competition.'

'I thought you sent *Carousel's* picture,' said Pete, 'not your own.'

'Don't be silly, darling,' twittered his partner. 'You know what I mean.' She lifted Carousel out of her chair and whirled her round the kitchen, singing:

'How fantastic, oh how grand
Prettiest daughter in the land
Sparkling eyes and curly hair
Gonna be a *millionaire*.'

The letter had instructions. They must take their daughter to London, where she'd be presented with her prize and meet the boss of a top modelling agency. When the day came, Carousel was woken at dawn to be bathed, powdered and stuffed into an expensive dress. Patricia brushed her hair till Carousel's eyes watered and then she got into trouble for making her mascara run. Her feet disappeared into a pair of fashionable shoes. There wasn't time for breakfast and, anyway, Patricia didn't want Carousel getting fat and spoiling her big chance.

In London everybody made a fuss of her. A famous pop star presented the thousand pounds and asked Carousel to marry him. He was just kidding, but Patricia thought it was wonderful. Flashbulbs popped all around, making the little girl blink. People shoved microphones at her and shouted questions she didn't understand. A twinkling Patricia answered for her. 'Yes, my daughter was amazed when she heard she'd won. Yes, she wants *desperately* to be a model: she's a natural in front of the camera, always was. Hobbies? Clothes and hair, doesn't play with other children: far too messy. No, she won't attend a local school when she's five, her heart's set on stage school, a career in films. No, she's *never* wanted to be just an ordinary, happy little girl.'

That's not true, thought Carousel, *I do want to be ordinary. I want to play out like the other kids. Go to their parties, have them to mine. I hate cameras, hate clothes, hate hair. Love mud and dust and charging about, throwing things and screeching.*

It was no use, though. The head of the model agency fell for the little girl at once. 'Carousel Cockcroft,' he beamed, 'you're gonna be the biggest little girl in the world. You'll be the Spice Girls, Lara Croft and Harry Potter, all rolled into one. Why – even the *name's* perfect.'

The Cockcrofts were whisked across London straightaway to the studio of a famous fashion photographer. There, Carousel was hustled in and out of a succession of outfits from somebody's autumn collection. The photographer snapped away busily, all the time calling out instructions to the dizzy three-year-old. 'Lift the head, darling. Bit more. Now gimme the smile. That's it.' *Click click click*. 'Now turn slowly, look straight into the camera.' *Click click click*. 'Lovely.' It seemed to go on for hours. Pete and Patricia had been taken off somewhere for coffee. Carousel didn't like coffee, but she'd have loved a glass of juice or even water. It wasn't offered. Under the hot lights she turned and posed and pouted, till at last the photographer said, 'OK, sweetie-pie, that's a wrap and you're a star.'

*

'How was it, darling?' smiled Patricia as the Cockcrofts clambered into a waiting taxi.

Carousel's throat was dry and she had a headache. 'I hated it, Mummy. *Hated* it.'

'Nonsense, darling, how can you say such a thing? All those pretty clothes!'

'But they're not *mine*, Mummy. I don't want to do that any more.'

'Don't be silly, darling – you're just tired. Besides, the nice man gave Daddy and me a contract to sign. You belong to him now, as well as to Daddy and me.'

It was true. They hadn't been home more than a couple of days when the phone rang and they went dashing off to Newcastle so that Carousel could model nine outfits on the riverbank with a famous bridge behind her. It was a drizzly day, but they made it look sunny with lights and blowdried Carousel's hair at every change. She was being paid a lot of money for the day's work, and the nice man was paying Pete and Patricia too, as chaperones, but she didn't care. She wished she was in the park at home, on the swings, licking an ice lolly. Money's not exciting when you're three.

And so it went on. Carousel's face was in glossy magazines, on billboards, in newspapers. She was interviewed on TV and had her own web site. She flew with Patricia and Pete to Spain, to France, to Italy. 'We're *so* lucky,' murmured Pete, 'so very lucky.' He and

Patricia had given up their jobs to travel with their daughter.

Carousel was cross. 'It's all right for you and Mum. You sit in the sun drinking fruit juice and looking at the scenery while I get hot and sticky under those awful lights. I've been to Spain and France and Italy but I haven't *seen* them. All I see is lights and silly clothes.'

'Don't be ungrateful, poppet,' said Pete. 'There are a million little girls out there wishing they were Carousel Cockcroft.'

And one who wishes she wasn't, thought Carousel.

She opened a shopping mall, made a CD with a top band and advertised a tasty new snack on TV. She wasn't allowed snacks herself in case they made her fat, but children everywhere pestered their parents for the crispy bar which would make them more like Carousel Cockcroft.

A year went by, then another, and another. Carousel had been all over the world. Money was piling up in the bank. To everybody else she was the Spice Girls, Lara Croft and Harry Potter all rolled into one, but to herself she was washed out, lonely and desperately unhappy.

One day, on a hillside in Greece where it was high summer, Carousel posed in front of a broken column and thought, *I can't do this any more*. She was seven. There was no shade, just glare that seared the eyes. Lizards baked on sizzling stones, slim fir trees sweated

resin. The sun threatened to cook the child's brain and the photographer still wanted lights. At the foot of the slope stood a caravan, oven-hot. Inside, a bad-tempered woman waited to dress Carousel for the seventh time, blot the sweat off her face and do her hair. She didn't like Greece and she detested children. Carousel especially. She'd find sly ways to twist and nip as she went about her work.

Carousel posed for six hours, and when Pete and Patricia came in a taxi to take her to the airport she had a splitting headache. 'How was your day, darling?' crooned Patricia, who looked cool and rested.

'Same as always,' said Carousel. 'What about yours?'

'Heavenly, darling.' She smiled dreamily, sighed. 'The sea, so *unbelievably* blue. And that divine little breeze saved our lives, didn't it, Pete?'

Pete nodded. 'We'd have frizzled without it.' He grinned. 'Hope it turns up in Casablanca.'

Carousel was due to model in Casablanca next week. She didn't say anything, just smiled out of the window.

They were late landing, so everybody was in a rush. By the time Pete, Patricia and Carousel approached the moving belt it was unreachable behind a trolley jam. Pete dodged about, craning over people's shoulders, watching the bags and looking for a space at the same time. He still hadn't found one when their luggage appeared. He seized Carousel's arm and shoved her into a gap between two trolleys. 'Go on,' he urged, 'push through and grab 'em: I'm too wide.'

Carousel squeezed through the gap, but instead of grabbing the bags she sat down on the belt, swung her legs clear of the floor and rode away. Pete yelled, 'What d'you think you're *doing*, you silly child?' and set off, barging through the crush, trying to keep up. Patricia, who'd slipped away to powder her nose, returned in time to see her little girl disappearing through the exit hatch. She screamed. 'Stop the belt – my *child* – somebody stop the belt!'

'No *don't* stop it, you daft woman,' cried Pete, 'she'll come round again.'

But she didn't.

A security man came running. A door was unlocked, baggage-handlers questioned. Nobody had noticed a child on the belt. An hysterical Patricia was led away by hospitality staff. Pete trailed after a squad of security guards as they began a thorough search, but Carousel was never found. She'd appeared by magic and she vanished by magic, and when Pete and Patricia finally crept home they found the snapshots gone too, and all the money. They went to bed and cried themselves to sleep, and when Patricia gave birth to a baby girl the following year, she dreamed a future for the child which had old dungarees in it, and dirt and fun and lots of sticky friends.

There might even be a worm or two.

WHEN THE FUNFAIR COMES TO TOWN

by Wes Magee
illustrated by Lauren Child

See the coloured lights that flash,
hear the dodgems when they crash,
give the coconuts a bash
when the funfair comes to town.

Smell the burgers, chips and pies,
wear a mask with wobbly eyes,
throw a hoop and win a prize
when the funfair comes to town.

See the crowds come in and out,
   hear the children scream and shout,
      climb aboard the roundabout
         when the funfair comes to town.

Cinder toffee – taste and share,
   hear loud music in the air,
      ride the ghost train . . . if you dare
         when the funfair comes to town.

THE MAGIC FAIRGROUND

by Laurence Anholt
illustrated by John Burningham

In a secret sunlit valley,
By a twisting mountain stream,
Suddenly the magic fairground
Lies before you like a dream.

Can you see the wheels and towers?
Smell the straw and coconut?
But a fence lies all around it
And the wooden gate is shut.

Finding something in your pocket,
Seems to be a golden key;
Open up the painted doorway,
Step inside and you are free.

Welcome to the magic fairground
Where the colours seem so bright,
Where the music makes you giddy,
Where the rides go on all night.

Music from a band of monkeys
Dancing to a wild guitar;
Drive a million miles an hour
In your dashing dodgem car.

Climb aboard the helter-skelter,
Winding up the wooden stair;
Climb so high you meet a moonman,
Stardust sparkling in your hair.

Corkscrew road of gleaming silver,
Flying on a prickly mat,
Swirling, whirling, twirling, curling,
Landing almost knocks you flat.

Round and round the magic fairground
Where a juggler walks on wire,
Where the world is made of canvas,
Where a strongman swallows fire.

Feeling just a little hungry,
See a stiltman through the crowd;
Stretches up into the sunset,
Hands you down a sugar cloud.

Step inside the Hall of Mirrors,
Cloudfloss melting on your tongue;
Mirrors make a baby ancient,
Mirrors make the old folk young.

Barefoot bouncing on the castle,
Somersaulting through the sky;
Feeling light as floating pollen,
Feeling you can really fly.

Round and round the magic fairground
Where the flagpoles scrape the sky,
Where a strange man sleeps on nails,
Where the coconuts are shy.

Ancient gypsy with a crystal,
'Come and have your fortune told!'
Says your life is like a fairground,
Can you find the key of gold?

Standing sadly in the moonlight,
Has the time slipped by so fast?
One more ride is waiting for you,
You have saved the best till last.

Clamber on this racing dragon,
Fire leaping from its snout;
You can ride on any creature
On the rushing roundabout.

Round and round the magic fairground
Where the children laugh and scream,
Where the ride goes on forever,
Where the world is just a dream.

You could ride a racing pony,
Sit astride a bumblebee,
Clinging tightly to a tiger,
Dive on dolphins through the sea.

Stretching up to reach the treasure,
Jumps away each time you try;
Will you have to leave with nothing?
Feel yourself begin to cry.

Then you see a friendly giant
Bowing with a little laugh.
'I will help you reach the treasure,'
Says the gentle green giraffe.

Round and round the magic fairground
Fingers reaching for the prize;
A golden key is what you find there
And you can't believe your eyes!

So at last you leave the fairground,
Past the winding, sparkly stream;
Hear the doorway close behind you.
Was it all a lovely dream?

In the secret, sunlit valley
On the never-ending lane;
Finding something in your pocket
And the tale begins again.

ALEXANDER'S RAGTIME CAT

by **Jan Mark**
illustrated by **Ken Brown**

There was a miller and he had three sons. The eldest was called Albert and he drove the donkey cart to carry sacks of grain to the mill.

The second son was called Alfred and he drove the donkey cart to carry sacks of flour to the baker.

The youngest son was called Alexander and he did everything else.

Times were hard and the miller was old. One day he sat down at his desk to make his will. While he was writing, the cat walked in.

'What will become of the boys when I have gone?' the miller sighed.

'I dare say they'll get by,' the cat said, and jumped on to the desk. 'What are you writing?'

'My will,' said the miller. 'Can't you read?'

'Of course not, I'm a cat,' the cat said. It went over to the piano and played a few bars of *Für Elise*, by Beethoven, the twiddly bit in the middle. 'What's the problem?'

'I have nothing to leave but the mill, the donkey and the cart.'

'Simple enough,' the cat said. 'Three things to leave and three people to leave them to.'

'But suppose they quarrel?' the miller said. 'The cart is no use without the donkey, the donkey is no use without the cart and the mill will be no use without either.'

'You should have brought them up not to quarrel,' the cat said. 'And I wish you'd take better care of this piano. The mice have been at the sheet music again.'

'Isn't that your department?' the miller said. 'What would you suggest?'

'Leave the mill to Albert, leave the donkey and cart to Alfred, and leave me to Alexander,' the cat said. 'And while you're at it, you can leave the piano to me.'

'Fair enough,' the miller said, too tired to argue. He made his will neatly on a clean sheet of paper. 'Could you witness it for me?' he said.

'Of course I can't, I'm a cat,' the cat said. It arched its back and launched into Tchaikovsky's Piano Concerto No. 1.

Soon after that the miller turned up his toes and died. When the funeral was over, his three sons went back to the mill and the family lawyer came to read the will.

The boys sat in a row on the sofa, the lawyer sat at the miller's desk and the cat sat on the piano stool.

The lawyer read the will aloud. 'I leave my mill to

my eldest son Albert. I leave the donkey and cart to my second son Alfred. I leave the cat to my youngest son Alexander. I leave the piano to the cat.'

'Cats can't inherit pianos,' Albert said. 'You might as well leave it the mill.'

'What would I do with a mill?' the cat asked. 'I'm a cat.' It twirled round on the piano stool and began to play the 'Dead March' from *Saul*, by Handel.

'Don't I get anything else?' Alexander said.

'There's nothing else to get,' Albert said. He went off to the pub with Alfred.

'Drinking the profits,' the cat remarked. 'They won't last long if they carry on like that.'

'What am I going to do?' Alexander said.

'Get a good night's sleep,' the cat said. 'I have plans for us.'

Alexander climbed to his bed in the little room above the donkey's stable. He fell asleep watching the stars through the window and hearing the cat play Brahms's 'Lullaby'.

Next morning two men came with a wagon and took the piano away.

'What are you doing with my piano?' the cat said.

'Selling it,' Albert said, tossing coins in his hand.

'Do I get the proceeds?' the cat said.

'Don't make me laugh,' Albert said. 'You're a cat.' He went off to the pub with Alfred and kicked the cat as he went past.

'Now what do we do?' Alexander said.

'We pick me up and stroke me and say, "Poor

Puss," ' the cat said, 'because I have been kicked. Then we set out to seek our fortune.'

'I suppose you are going to find me a king's daughter to marry,' Alexander said, bitterly.

'What have you been reading?' the cat said. 'Don't be ridiculous, we are going to Leeds.'

Alexander knew better than to argue. He went away and packed his few possessions in a bag. Then he said goodbye to the donkey and went to meet the cat, which was sitting on the doorstep, washing its tail.

When it saw Alexander, it stood up and walked down the lane without a backward glance, but Alexander turned his head all the way as he looked his last on the mill that had been his home all his life.

As they passed the pub, Albert and Alfred looked out of the window and shouted rude remarks. Alexander tried not to listen but the cat had no trouble ignoring them. It was a cat.

At the end of the lane they turned on to the main road.

'Why are we going to Leeds?' Alexander asked.

'Every three years in Leeds,' said the cat, 'there is a world-famous piano competition. Everyone has heard of it, except you. I happen to know that it is being held at this very moment.'

'I don't think that listening to a piano competition would cheer me up,' Alexander said.

'We are not going there so that you can listen to

it,' the cat said. 'We are going there so that I can win it.'

'Do you think you have a chance?' Alexander said.

'Even if I do not win first prize, the greatest critics in Europe will be there,' the cat said. 'I am sure to be offered engagements.'

'Because you're a cat?'

'Because I am an artiste,' the cat said. 'This is a musical contest, not a freak show.'

They walked another mile.

'Are we going all the way on foot?' Alexander said.

'We are going by train,' the cat said, 'but it is still six miles to the station. You had better carry me for a while, I have to take care of my paws.'

Alexander put the cat over his shoulder and it practised five-claw exercises up and down his back.

When they reached the station, the cat said, 'Go and ask how much it will cost to travel to Leeds.'

The man at the ticket office told Alexander that it would cost him thirty-five pounds just to get to Leeds and much more to come back again.

Alexander went and told the cat. 'But cats travel free,' Alexander said.

'Have you got thirty-five pounds?' the cat asked.

'I have five pounds in all the world,' Alexander said.

'In that case I shall have to travel alone,' the cat said. 'Cross the road to that hardware shop and buy me a basket.'

The basket cost four pounds and twenty-five

pence. Alexander went back to the station and the cat climbed into the basket.

'When is the Leeds train due to leave?' the cat said.

'In ten minutes,' Alexander said. 'It is standing at Platform Two.'

'Get me aboard,' the cat said. 'I think I should prefer a First Class carriage.'

Alexander carried the cat on board and found an empty carriage.

'Put the basket on the luggage rack,' the cat said, climbing out. 'If the train becomes crowded and I am occupying a seat people could turn unpleasant and there might be questions asked.'

Alexander put the basket on the rack while the cat looked out of the window.

'I see a newsagent's stall,' the cat said. 'Perhaps you could buy me a newspaper.'

'Which one would you like,' Alexander said, 'the *Daily Post*, the *Morning Sun* or the *Evening Star*?'

'The *Sun* sounds nice and warm,' the cat said, so Alexander went to buy a copy.

When he got back to the train he said, 'How long will you be away?'

'For as long as it takes,' the cat said.

'What shall I do?' Alexander asked.

'Wait,' the cat said. 'Wait here. I'm sure you can earn your keep doing odd jobs around the station. You might even try singing in the street. Your voice isn't trained but it's pleasant enough.'

Then the whistle blew. Alexander jumped out of the train. As it began to move he put his head in at the window and said, 'Goodbye, good luck.'

'I hardly imagine I shall need luck,' the cat said, 'but thank you for thinking of it.'

Alexander stood on Platform Two and waved until the train was out of sight, but long before Alexander was out of sight the cat opened its newspaper, curled up on it and went to sleep.

When the train pulled in at the next station, the cat woke up, looked out of the window and saw many people on the platform. To be on the safe side it sprang to the luggage rack and sat in its basket. However, no one was travelling First Class and when the train started again the cat climbed out. But just as it was about to jump down on to the seat, two shifty-looking men sidled in.

Hah! Second Class passengers, if not Third, the cat thought.

The men sat down. One of them picked up the *Morning Sun*.

'Excuse me,' the cat said, descending, 'but that is my newspaper.'

The two men looked extremely surprised.

'Did you speak?' said one.

'You have taken my newspaper,' the cat said.

'You *did* speak,' said the second shifty man.

'Be so good as to return it,' the cat said.

'Doing the crossword, was you?' said the first shifty man, and he winked meaningly at the second man.

'Of course not, I'm a cat,' the cat said.

The second man winked at the first man. 'Are you thinking what I'm thinking?'

'Could be a lot of money in a talking cat.'

'I am a musician,' the cat said, but the first man grabbed the basket in one hand and the cat in the other, and stuffed the cat into the basket.

The second man tied a piece of string round the basket to keep the lid shut. The cat put its claws through a gap and drew blood, but the men only laughed in a sarcastic manner.

'Try that again and you'll be sorry,' the first man said.

'I doubt it,' said the cat. 'If you want to make money out of a talking cat you'd better make sure the cat wants to talk.'

At the next station but one the men took the basket and the newspaper and left the train.

'Are we in Leeds?' the cat said.

'What do you want to go to Leeds for?' the first man said.

'I have business there,' the cat said.

'Wrong,' the second man said. 'You have business here. That is, *we* have business here and you are it.'

'I refuse to do business with you,' the cat said, 'and if you think you can make me cooperate, you do not know much about cats.'

'You're alive, aren't you?' the first man said. 'I know all about things that are alive. Most of them want to stay alive.'

'Empty threats,' the cat said to itself. 'There is not a lot of money in a dead cat.' It looked through the gap under the lid of the basket. The men were walking down grimy streets, past shuttered shops, boarded-up doors and warehouses with rows of broken windows – very gloomy.

The light was failing. Rain began to fall. Criminal-looking persons peered around corners while burglars said goodbye to their wives and children and set off to work.

At last they came to a run-down theatre with old posters hanging off the walls. The men went inside where it was very dark and smelled of damp. The cat could hear mice running about.

'I hope you are not expecting me to catch rodents,' the cat said. 'I have to look after my paws.'

'Shut up,' the first man said. 'Your turn to talk will come in a minute. And you'd better speak up.'

The second man knocked on a door with a sign saying MANAGER tacked to it. A beery voice yelled, 'Come in!'

On the other side of the door was an office where a man sat behind a desk with his feet on it.

'Oh, it's you, is it?' he said. 'I don't know what you've got in that basket but I told you before, I'm not interested in performing dogs, performing rats, performing sheep or performing fleas. I do not want to meet Zippo the Wonder Tortoise or Conan the Super Bunny, or the Incredible Shrinking Newt.

I've had it up to here with horses that can count to ten, parrots that can predict the lottery, ferrets that can foretell the weather –'

'You think we've got a horse in here?' the first man said, tapping the basket.

'No, I doubt it's a horse. It's a frog, isn't it? It's a Sagacious Frog. I've had it up to here with Sagacious Frogs.'

The second man gave the basket a vicious prod. 'Say something.'

'Miaou,' the cat said.

'Oh, it's a cat. What does it do – no, let me guess. It can whistle "Land of My Fathers" while riding a unicycle. It does synchronized swimming.'

'It talks,' the second man said.

'I heard it. It said miaou. I've got a very old mog out by the stage door can say that.'

The first man made sure that the door was shut and untied the basket. He did not notice that the dirty window was open a crack at the top.

The cat shot out of the basket, ran up the curtains and shouted out of the window, 'Help! Police! I am being held against my will!'

The second man started to pull the cat down again by its tail. Much blood was shed.

'All right,' the manager said, when the cat was wrapped around his head with its claws in his neck, 'that is certainly a talking cat. I believe you. What else can it say?'

The cat hissed in the manager's ear, 'Get those

two crooks out of here and we'll talk.'

'You heard it,' the manager said. 'Out. Leave the premises.'

The two men went off, muttering. The cat made itself comfortable in the 'pending' tray and washed its paws.

'They don't own me, you know,' the cat said. 'I was hijacked.'

'Who does own you?'

'I own myself. I live with Alexander Millerson who is waiting for me at the station.'

'Which station?'

'How should I know? I'm a cat.'

'You could be famous,' the manager said.

'I intend to be,' the cat said. 'I was on my way to Leeds to take part in the piano competition.'

'You can play the piano as well?'

'As well as what?' the cat said. 'I don't have any other instrument. When I retire from the keyboard, I shall probably take up conducting.'

'What do you play?' the manager asked.

'At Leeds I meant to give them some Schumann, and perhaps a little Beethoven. The 'Moonlight' Sonata always goes down well.'

'I don't think it will go down very well here,' the manager said. 'But take my word for it,' he added, craftily, 'you'd be wasting your time in Leeds. Concert pianists are two a penny. The big money's in jazz.'

'Jazzzzz?' the cat said, with a hiss. 'Listen, sunshine, it's Beethoven or it's miaou. Take your pick.'

'I'll put you on at the end of the first half tonight,' the manager said. 'You'll soon find out what the public wants.'

'First half of what?' the cat said.

'First half of the bill. You can go on after the sword-swallower. I suppose you wouldn't like to say a few words before you start?'

'I am not appearing as a talking cat,' the cat said. 'I am a pianist, take it or leave it. In the meantime you can get me something to eat.'

'After the show,' the manager said. 'Hunger adds an edge to a performance.'

'Hunger adds an edge to my claws,' the cat said.

'I'll send in some milk,' the manager said, as he went out, but first he fastened the window and he locked the door behind him.

'These people think I am an idiot,' the cat said to itself. 'But I am a cat.'

That evening the manager carried the basket backstage and the cat had to listen to a large lady singing off-key, a small man telling terrible jokes and someone playing a ukulele. Through the gap under the lid of the basket the cat watched a young person spinning plates, and then the sword-swallower came on. The cat noticed that the audience did not clap very much but threw a great many tomatoes at the stage.

'Your turn now,' the manager said, when the sword-swallower left the stage in a hurry.

The cat walked over to the piano and looked at the audience.

'If you wish to throw anything, I suggest you make it fish,' it said. Then it leaped on to the piano stool and flexed its claws.

After five bars of Beethoven's 'Moonlight' Sonata the first tomato hit the piano.

'Rubbish!' someone shouted, out in the darkness, but the cat played on.

'Give us something with a tune!' bawled another dissatisfied customer as a second tomato went by.

No point in wasting fine music on people with tin ears, the cat thought.

'I shall now play "Way Down Upon the Swannee River",' it said, over its shoulder, and changed key.

Five bars into 'Way Down Upon the Swannee River' the third tomato arrived.

'Very well,' the cat sighed. 'Get your lugholes round this, you Philistines.'

It jumped on to the keyboard and began playing with all four feet: 'Maple Leaf Rag', 'Pineapple Rag', 'Tiger Rag' and 'Twelfth Street Rag'. The rain of tomatoes ceased, the audience rose to its feet, clapping and calling for more.

As a final encore the cat gave them 'Hiawatha', running up and down the keys at speed from bass to treble. At last the manager called for the curtain to fall, at which the cat sprang from the piano, over the footlights and vanished into the auditorium.

'Stop that cat!' the manager yelled, but no one could find it in the darkness. By the time the house

lights went up, the cat had zigzagged between feet from the front to the back, and left the theatre.

'Get yourself a proper job,' it said to the stage-door tabby as it went by.

The cat made its way to the station and boarded the first train going south. This time it travelled under the seats to be on the safe side, and counted the stations. When the train stopped for the third time, it got out and went to look for Alexander.

Alexander had waited patiently for his cat to return, for it was all he had in the world. The cat found him standing in the rain outside the station, singing to passers-by who sometimes gave him money and sometimes did not.

'Oh, I'm so glad to see you,' Alexander said, when the cat walked out of the station. 'Did you win?'

'How much have you made?' the cat said, ignoring the question.

'Five pounds – and a few pennies left over from when I bought the basket. How did you get on in Leeds?'

'I did not go to Leeds,' the cat said. 'I had a better idea. Take your money and buy a ticket to London.'

'London!' cried Alexander. 'Where the streets are paved with gold?'

'As far as I know they are paved with concrete,' the cat said.

'What are we going to do in London?'

'I am going to get a recording contract,' the cat said, 'and you can be my manager.'

'Why do you need a manager?' Alexander said.

'Do me a favour,' the cat said. 'How can I possibly manage my own affairs? I am a cat.'

CAROUSEL –
THE HORSE'S SONG

by Judith Nicholls
illustrated by Paul Geraghty

An untamed spirit in disguise,
though I'm no rebel runaway
yet still I reach for soaring skies.

I have my lows, I have my highs,
as any long-time captive may;
an untamed spirit in disguise.

No winds will ever hear my sighs
for sighs and cries are not my way,
but still I reach for soaring skies.

Though tethered tightly from sunrise
I dance with joy through blue or grey,
an untamed spirit in disguise.

The circling world spins past my eyes,
a pot-pourri of disarray;
I only reach for soaring skies.

Escape, maybe, would be unwise
but dreams like mine will not
    decay;
an untamed spirit in disguise,
one day I'll reach the
    soaring skies.

COME TO THE FAIR

by Joan Aiken
illustrated by Ruth Brown

GAY and glorious, one day every year, the market square of this little town is, and that's the day in September when the fair comes, and music peals, and roundabouts whirl, and the through traffic, if it wants to get by, has to give the town a miss and scrape along side lanes past sodden blackberry hedges. Though where through traffic should be going don't ask me, for beyond the town, up the mountain, stands nothing but the water tower, on its one leg like a broody heron, and the castle of Owen Richards the poet. Beyond again, and all round for that matter, lie only the mountains, heaving their mossy shoulders into the rain and the mist.

On Fair Day, then, the big roundabout takes up all the centre of the town square with its horses and swans and dragons, while round it, thick as currants in a birthday cake, crowd the sideshows and stalls and rifle galleries, not to mention Jones the Rope

Trick, the lovely fortune-telling Myfanwy and, this year we are speaking of, Señor Pedro.

Señor Pedro was a wizened little man, nose like a parrot, eyes like chips of anthracite, hair a mere wisp at the back of his head and a walnut-shell face that was wrinkled and seemed as if he slept face down on a doormat every night.

Indeed, he was talking about his face, standing on a big box in front of his little tent. The box was wreathed about with pink paper, and on the tent hung a banner:

Agua de Vida, Water of Life

'You see my face, señores, señoras?' he was shouting to the crowd. 'Wrinkled, you think, my friends, but you are wrong. My face was scratched by thorns, yes, thorns – those very thorns that the South American pygmies use to tip their arrows. On the slopes of the Andes, your honours, grows a terrible thorn thicket, many miles across. In the middle of this thicket is a spring. Ah, your honours, such a beautiful spring! Nowhere in the world is there one like it – this is the spring of the water of youth. One sip removes twenty, thirty years from your age.'

'A fine story to tell us, that is!' shouted a derisive voice. 'Why hasn't anyone ever heard of this water before?'

Shrugging a patient shoulder, Señor Pedro replied, 'Am I not telling you, señoras, señores? This water is very hard to procure. The Indians are hostile, the place is distant, the thicket is impenetrable and perilous, *muy periculoso*.'

'If the water does that to you, why don't the Indians drink it and stay young forever?'

'*Quien sabe?* Maybe they do. Who can tell what age a pygmy has reached? But what I am come to tell you, señoras, is that with me I have –' here he brought it from under his jacket and held it up with a flourish, '– a bottle, the last bottle in Europe, of this renowned, miraculous, youth-giving liquid brought to you all the way from Brazil.' There was a murmur of wonder from the crowd, and they gazed at the stone bottle, which was crowned with gold foil and might hold a quart.

'Why don't you drink it yourself?' shrilled Mrs Griffith the Dispensary. 'Poison I believe it is!'

'Ah, that's probable! Or why should he be offering it for sale when he's as worn and wizened himself as an old seed potato?'

'Maybe he prefers the money – fair play,' suggested Rhys the Red Dragon.

'Why should I wish to grow younger?' said Señor Pedro scornfully. 'One life with its troubles is enough for me. I have all I need. Back in the Andes my good wife is waiting for me, beautiful as an angel. But the dearest longing of her heart is a new grand piano, for though we stood the legs of her Otway in four pans of kerosene, the termites ate it away until nothing remained but the keys.'

'Did you ever hear of such a calamity?' mourned the sympathetic crowd.

'Her only wish is to play once more. And that is why, señoras, señores, at risk to my life, I filled six bottles with the water of youth and came to Europe. Here you see the last of them. I am now going to auction it. Will any gracious lady or gentleman offer me five hundred pounds for it, this miraculous elixir, this water of youth?'

'Come on now, Lily Griffith! Tickled to death your old man would be, to see you a lovely young twenty-one-year-old again!'

'As if I'd waste my money on such stuff,' sniffed Mrs Griffith. 'Better things I have to do with it. Five hundred pounds indeed!' The crowd hesitated, broke, laughed and bargained. Señor Pedro kept the auction bubbling like a lukewarm kettle.

There were other attractions in the square. Music thundered between the houses, there were goldfish to be won by a skilful fling of a dart, hot dogs to be eaten, vases and tea sets at the rifle gallery, candyfloss for the children; and all the time the rain pelted down. But the great shafts of light pushing upwards from the sideshows turned the rain to a canopy of sparkle.

Owen Richards the poet came down from his castle to the fair with Ariel his guest; a famous actress from the boards of London, and the love of his long life.

'I must have my fortune told,' said she, making a

beeline for Myfanwy's van with its sugar-pink stripes and the portrait of Myfanwy over the door which had so bewitched Ianto Evans two years before that he had gone into the van and never been seen again.

'You should, at least, have no worries about your fortune, Ariel,' said Owen, but she shuddered as she glanced into a little shell-encrusted looking glass that he had won at the rifle gallery and caught a glimpse of her lovely, ageing face. He followed her into the sugar-striped van.

Myfanwy was playing waterfalls with a pack of cards which she could pour from one hand to the other like water from a cup to a can.

'Tell my fortune,' commanded Ariel, and she put out her hand.

'Steady you must hold it, then,' Myfanwy bade her, and she built a card-house on Ariel's palm: ten, jack, queen, king and the ace for a roof; Ariel neither budged nor spoke.

'Second storey it is,' Myfanwy said at that, and she built another on top of the first. Ariel held her hand steady as a table – a fine, thin hand, and the wrist so transparent you could see the veins in it. 'Fancy now,' Myfanwy said, and she laid a third storey on top of the second. 'Very unusual that is.'

But still the tower stood without falling on Ariel's palm, and Myfanwy pursed her lips and added the final storey, four black spades and the ace on top of it all.

'Now blow,' she said, and Ariel blew, scattering

the cards like a shower of apple blossom across the tent. Myfanwy picked them up. A look of amazement came over her face. 'O dammo,' said she, 'crazy old fortune you've got here. Neither head nor tail can I make of it! Try again, you must.'

'No, I'll not try again,' said Ariel, laughing. 'I'm not wishful to tempt providence too far. We'll leave it at that.' And she crossed Myfanwy's hand with a flourish of half-crowns.

'Can't you say if she'll marry?' asked Owen

Richards the poet, anxious as a hen with one duckling.

'Far as I can make out she'll have more husbands than Henry the Eighth,' Myfanwy said. 'A heron must have flown over the van and bewitched the cards. Good luck to you, lady, and remember Myfanwy in your will.'

Ariel laughed. 'Maybe I'll never make a will,' she said. Out they went into the rain again.

Soon as they were gone, Ianto Evans, he that had left his good wife for Myfanwy's sake two years before, crept out from under the bed.

'Ten o'clock,' he said. 'Blodwen will have been out to Jones the Cod to buy her bit of fish and chips. Locked away snug, she'll be, watching the telly; I'll just nip along home and dig up the clematis by the back door. Planted that clematis myself, I did; no reason it shouldn't come with us on our wanderings. Lovely little flowers it has, like red butterflies.'

'Careful now, Ianto *bach*,' Myfanwy said. 'Supposing she's out at the fair? Meet her you might, and then the fur would fly.'

'Not Blodwen, not her. She never went to a fair since the day she was old enough to pop a penny into a money box.' And off he strode into the silvery wet night, and went sniffing up the alley to his back door like a hound on a fish trail – only he was on the track of Blodwen and her Friday four-penn'orth, to make sure she was safely locked up with the hake and chips. Smell of fish there was, sure enough, but it had been left by Thomas the Electric, four houses further on. Just put the clematis in his pocket, Ianto had, when Blodwen came along with her supper and let out a screech at the sight of him.

'Oh, there's my skulking husband that ran off and left me for a cardsharping Jezebel! Wait till I get my hands on you, Ianto my man!'

Ran he did, like a hare, and she after him, down the alley, through the coconut shies, into the square, past the learned pig, between the tenpins, up the skittle alley and three times round the hot-dog stand. Towards Myfanwy's van he fled, meaning perhaps to hide behind her skirts, and then, gaining a bit of sense before it was too late, turned aside into Jones the Rope Trick's enclosure. 'Save me, Jones man, save me!' he bawled.

The crowd cheered and laughed, for most of them had felt the weight of Blodwen's tongue at one time or another, and they were on the side of the underdog. Quick as a wink, Jones picked up his clarinet and tootled out 'Men of Harlech'. The coiled rope stood up and begged like a hamadryad; no monkey ever climbed quicker than Ianto shinned up it, hand over hand. When Blodwen arrived, ten quick seconds later by Morgan the Turf's stopwatch, he was out of sight into the black, wet sky above.

'Gone he has, ma'am,' said Jones, very sober.

'Angels are singing "Cwm Rhondda" round him this minute, likely as not.'

Blodwen gave Jones one look, one, but enough to loosen every stopping in his teeth, and then she turned on her heel and started for home; she knew when she was beaten. But on her way, having lost her hake and chips in the chase, she stopped at the stand for a hamburger and tomato sauce.

Meanwhile, Señor Pedro had sold his Water of Youth to Ariel the actress for two hundred and seventy pounds, nine shillings and ninepence. 'Only to such a lovely lady as you would I part with my precious water for so mean a sum,' he mourned, handing over the gold-wrapped bottle.

'There's crazy for you!' said Mrs Griffith. 'Fancy spending all that good money on an old bottle with like as not nothing but tap water inside it.'

'Try a drop!' shouted the crowd.

'Throw it away!' begged Owen Richards the poet. 'Marry me, Ariel! Forget about the moribund old theatre. Stay here! Queen of the whole town you'd be.'

But Ariel looked about at the crowd, and in her voice that could sing or whisper its way up to the tip-top seat in the gallery she called, 'Who can lend me a corkscrew?'

Morgan the Turf had his whipped out, a photo finish ahead of Rhys the Red Dragon. He took the bottle, and opened it with a bow.

Set her lips to it, then, Ariel did, and a quick

swallow with her. Then she stopped, half laughing, half scared, crying, 'Dare I go on?'

'Throw it away, Ariel love,' Owen Richards begged.

But the crowd shouted, 'Drink up, ma'am!'

Now a law of physics there is, see, very unbreakable, which says, 'All that goes up must come down.' And just at that moment what should come down but Ianto Evans like an old blockbuster, plump into the middle of things. Knocked the bottle clean out of Ariel's hand he did – lucky she'd put the cork back – and himself pretty near silly. Soon on his feet again he was, though, for when Blodwen, teeth halfway through her hamburger, loitering to enjoy a free spectacle for once in her cheeseparing life, laid eyes on him, she was after him again like an old pike after a springtime salmon. Off into the dark alleys he fled, clasping the bottle in his frantic hand. Once he tripped and fell and dropped it; Blodwen swooped on him, but it was the bottle she grabbed in her haste, not Ianto.

'Oh, but I'll have you yet,' shouted the termagant, and while Morgan the Turf was going round laying two to one on Blodwen, the pair of them kept it up round the town, ding-dong, now here, now there.

No lie now, for many a long year after, if a man wanted to describe something faster than mere speed he'd say, 'Like Blodwen Evans the night she was after her husband Ianto.'

Meanwhile, what of Ariel?, you will be asking,

and indeed to goodness there was wonder enough in the way the years were dropping off her like layers of gauze. No more than nineteen she looked now, as she stood scared and smiling, and a long *ah!* at her beauty trembled through the crowd. Only Owen Richards in grief turned his head away; he knew she was lost to him forever now.

'Oh!' she cried, 'I'm afraid, I'm afraid of what is happening to me! Must it all begin again, the doubts and terrors of youth? Comfort me, Owen dear, tell me I haven't changed. Owen, comfort me!'

But he in silence held up to her the little shell-bordered looking glass. When she had looked once it seemed as if the weight of her beauty would crush her like a snowfall in May. Stepped away, she did, hanging her head, and the crowd parted in a hush as she walked to her car.

'Back to London, is it?' said Owen, standing with his hand on the bonnet.

'Back to London, indeed,' said she, sighing.

'Then goodbye, my love.'

Her tears splashed on the steering wheel like raindrops as she drove away to face her new legend of life and the harshness of being young. Owen, with a heart of lead, turned back, but with no spirit in him for the fair.

'Let's hope we've seen the last of that bottle; unsettling it is,' Rhys the Red Dragon commented.

And Mrs Griffith said, 'Indeed to goodness, yes!'

But Blodwen now, breathless, with tomato sauce

sticking in her gullet like china clay, had stopped the chase of Ianto a moment to take a swig at the bottle, hoping maybe – knowing her Ianto – that it would be whisky. But no more than a couple of good gollops had she taken ('*Ach y fi*, it's only water, then!') when she laid eyes on Ianto stealing back to Myfanwy's van behind the big roundabout.

Quick as a weasel after him, Blodwen. Over the roundabout she went, threading her way between horses and swans. 'Give us a break, Alun, man!' shouted Ianto.

'Start her up, then!' and Alun threw in his gears with a thrashing like an old whale in convulsions. Slow at first, then faster, spinning in a giddy gold spiral, switchbacking up and down, round went the swans and dragons, a whole glittering stableland of bucking broncos.

Well! Stuck fast Blodwen was, and had to make the best of it, clinging tight to a swan's neck. But the bottle, spun out of her hand by another natural wonder known as centrifugal force, flew off like a bullet over the heads of the crowd, and nobody's eye followed it into the dark.

Gone, and a good riddance too, Owen Richards thought. Back to his castle then, poor Mr Richards, to live out his final years with owls and ink, in an everlasting third act of spiderwebs. Or so he thought.

*

Sitting over a bottle of claret he was, late enough for tomorrow's moon, when half the town came tapping at his door, timid but trustful, for to whom but a poet can you turn when life throws up such a problem as the roundabout had tossed them?

'See here, Mr Richards *bach*, an orphan we have on our hands,' says Morgan the Turf, very solemn, and the crowd shoves forward a small girl, black-haired, sapling-thin, fierce as a fury.

'You're the wisest man in this town, Mr Richards dear,' the neighbours said. 'Fitting it is you should have charge of this child of misfortune. Too young she is to live in her own house alone, see; and her husband run off with the fortune-teller.'

'Husband?' said Owen Richards, and then he looked closer and recognized Blodwen Evans of forty years ago – Blodwen Pugh as she was then.

Tears of rage there were still on her cheeks, but forgetfulness had followed her plunge back into childhood. Her anger had left her and she gazed at him with no more than wonder for an old poet and his cobwebbed castle.

'Live with me, is it, my dear?' said Owen.

And she in awe answered, 'Yes, sir,' and bobbed a curtsy. Nodding approval, the town fathers withdrew to The Red Dragon.

Where, all this time, you will be asking, where is Señor Pedro, the author of these troubles?

Not a man to outstay his welcome, the little

pedlar, and he was tramping out of town down the rain-swept high road with his two hundred and seventy pounds when a speeding pink van overtook him.

'Lift to Cardiff?' called a head from the window – Ianto's.

'I thank you; yes.'

'Wet old night it is for walking,' Ianto said, as the little man unslung his pack and shook the mud out of his turn-ups.

'Indeed, yes.'

'No more of those bottles, have you?' Ianto asked, handing over a mug of tea and a hospitable wedge of cake, as Myfanwy drove them on their swift way.

Señor Pedro shook his head.

'Just as well then,' Ianto said. 'More trouble in that bottle than in a whole keg of whisky, if you will be asking my opinion.'

'You do not think that to grow younger is a blessing?'

'Not for Myfanwy and me.' And Ianto looked fondly at the back of Myfanwy's neck as she bent over the wheel. 'All we wish is that we grow old together and die on the same day.'

'Ah,' Señor Pedro said with sympathy, and he thought of his own dear wife on the slopes of the Andes.

What became of the bottle, you will be wondering, and the answer to that is easy: it fell into the town reservoir, standing on its one leg further up the mountainside. Put up the water rates like a shot, the council would have, had they guessed, but nobody did. Though, as the years went by, and no one in the place grew a day older, people did begin to wonder. But in a town the folk get used to one another's faces, and nobody thought about it very deeply as they went about their business. Visitors might have wondered at it indeed; become a famous tourist centre, the place might have, but for the seeds in Pedro's turn-ups.

Scattered some of those famous thorn seeds he had – whether by mistake or on purpose, who can say? – and almost overnight a dense thicket of brambles sprang up that soon had the town surrounded. Nobody noticed; too wrapped up in their own concerns they were, with council meetings and oratorios, weddings and Gorsedds, all presided over by Owen the poet and his happy adopted daughter Blodwen; Wales will hear of her too, one day, if copies of her poems ever find their way past the thorn thicket.

So there you have them: Ariel still a lovely legend on the boards of London town; Ianto and his Myfanwy, old and wrinkled and gay as two crickets travelling the country in their fortune-telling van, with the flowers of the clematis – its roots safely bedded in a pickle pot – fluttering like red butterflies over the roof; Señor Pedro long since back with his piano on the slopes of the Andes; the townspeople living their carefree unchanging lives till the Day of Judgement.

And what have any of them done to deserve it? Not a thing. No moral to this story, you will be saying, and I am afraid it is true.

SHE WAS A MERRY-GO-ROUND

by **Nick Toczek**

illustrated by **Satoshi Kitamura**

Oh, I lost my love on a carousel
To the whirling world and rich pell-mell
Of colour and sound and taste and smell
Of rides and stalls and the food they sell.

Yes, I lost my love on a carousel
When, under the fairground's magic spell,
She fell for a feckless ne'er-do-well
With blue tattoos and his hair in gel.

And I lost my love on a carousel
Cos the fortune-teller failed to tell
Me she was a jaded Jezebel
Who'd merrily bid me fond farewell
Then spin away on the carousel.

about the contributors

Joan Aiken (b. 1924) has published more than fifty books for adults and children. Her most successful children's books are those set in the imaginary time of James III, the first of which is *The Wolves of Willoughby Chase*. Her books for younger children include the hilarious adventures of an eccentric pet raven, Mortimer.

Nicholas Allan (b. 1956) trained at the Slade School of Art and worked in many different fields before his first picture book in 1989. *The Queen's Knickers* won the Picture Book category of the Sheffield Children's Award in 1994, and *Demon Teddy* won the Children's Book Award in 2000. His *Hilltop Hospital* TV series has had two BAFTA nominations as well as three international awards.

Laurence Anholt (b. 1959) is a prolific and versatile producer of children's books, many in partnership with his wife Catherine – including the *Chimp and Zee* titles. He has been awarded many prizes, including the Nestlé Smarties Gold Award twice. His series about great artists introduces young readers to the world of art. www.anholt.co.uk

Quentin Blake (b. 1932) was the first Children's Laureate (1999–2001). He records his experiences of those two years in *Laureate's Progress*. His illustration work is joyously anarchic. He was the first winner of the Children's Book Award in 1981 with *Mr Magnolia* and has received countless other awards from around the world including the 2002 Hans Christian Andersen Award for Illustration.

Ken Brown has worked in advertising and at the BBC as a graphic designer. He formed his own company in 1980 specializing in computer graphics, animation and live action. *Mucky Pup* won the Sheffield Children's Book Award in 1998.

Ruth Brown (b. 1941) has published about thirty books for children and has been shortlisted for the Kate Greenaway Medal several times, including *Snail Trail* in 2001. Her work is characterized by simple texts complemented by expansive and detailed illustrations. She is married to fellow artist Ken Brown.

Anthony Browne (b. 1946) is well known for his surreal (and sometimes controversial) imagery in picture books. Twice winner of the Kate Greenaway Medal (firstly with *Gorilla* in 1983) he has received countless awards from many countries. In 2000 he was honoured with the Hans Christian Andersen Award for his entire body of work.

John Burningham (b. 1936) began his illustration work designing posters for London Transport. He won his first Kate Greenaway Medal with his children's book, *Borka*, in 1963 and has won many awards since. Thirty years later he was invited to Japan and asked to write a story based upon the first steam locomotive exported there – *Oi! Get Off Our Train* was the result. He is married to fellow artist, Helen Oxenbury.

Emma Chichester Clark (b.1955) won the Mother Goose Award in 1988 as the most exciting newcomer to children's book illustration for *Listen to This*, a collection of short stories. Since then she has provided distinctive jackets for other authors and written and illustrated several picture books including *I Love You, Blue Kangaroo*, which was shortlisted for the Kate Greenaway Medal.

Lauren Child studied Illustration and then Mixed Media followed by an eclectic career including window displays, co-founding a lighting company and working in Damien Hirst's studio. Her individual style uses a combination of paint, photos, textiles, computer artwork and different typefaces. She won the 2000 Kate Greenaway Medal for *I Will Not Ever Never Eat a Tomato*.

Paul Cookson (b. 1961) used to be a teacher but is now a full-time poet who spends most of his time performing his work and leading workshops in schools. Paul has edited numerous anthologies, including *The Works*, as well as having two solo collections available. He listens to loud music while reading lots of books and watching football, and reviews for *Carousel*.

Gillian Cross (b. 1945) has been writing for readers of different ages since 1979. She describes herself as a storyteller and the power of story is evident in all her books. Her work has gathered many awards over the years including the Smarties Book Prize in 1992 for *The Great Elephant Chase*.

Joyce Dunbar (b. 1944) has written more than sixty books for children. She worked as a lecturer but since 1989 has been a full-time writer. She has collaborated with some of Britain's best-known illustrators on many successful picture books, including *Tell Me Something Happy Before I Go to Sleep*.

Polly Dunbar (b. 1977) is the artist/writer daughter of Joyce Dunbar. She trained at Brighton School of Art and is a rising star on the British illustration scene. Her most recent books include the *Hole Stories*, on *Cleopatra*, *Henry VIII* and *Scrooge*.

Michael Foreman (b. 1938) has illustrated more than thirty of his own books and over a hundred by other authors, particularly in collaboration with Michael Morpurgo. He has won numerous prizes including the Kate Greenaway Medal in 1989 for *War Boy*, the story of his own childhood.

John Foster (b.1941) taught for more than twenty years. Since 1988 he has concentrated on his writing as well as running workshops. He has written many school text books, but is now perhaps best known as a performance poet and editor of over a hundred poetry anthologies including *A Century of Children's Poems*. He is a regular reviewer for *Carousel*.

Paul Geraghty (b. 1959) was born and brought up in South

Africa. He travels across the world to see wildlife and different landscapes, which he used to great effect in *The Wonderful Journey* (1999). He has won the Earthworm Children's Book Award (1995) and the Children's Picture Book Award (1996).

Adèle Geras (b. 1944) is a former actor and teacher who now writes for all age groups. Her Jewish background is reflected in some of her writing, such as *My Grandmother's Stories*. She has published over eighty books for children – including the novel *Troy*, shortlisted for the Whitbread Children's Book of the Year 2002, and a ghost story for younger readers, *Goodbye Tommy Blue*. www.adelegeras.com

Mairi Hedderwick (b. 1939) trained at Edinburgh College of Art and has loosely based the ever popular *Katie Morag* picture books on the Isle of Coll where she lived for some years. Her books give children a vivid, unassuming and rare glimpse of life in rural Scotland. She also illustrates her adult travel books.

Harry Horse has been a political cartoonist, formed a bluegrass band and now not only writes and illustrates children's books, but provides cartoons for the *New Yorker* and writes and directs intricate computer games. His book *The Last Polar Bear* was made into a film in 2001.

Shirley Hughes (b. 1927) has an illustrative style which is distinctive, showing an obvious skill for observation. Her books about Alfie and Annie Rose are loved by generations of children. She was awarded the Eleanor Farjeon Award in 1984, an OBE in 1999 and was made a Fellow of the Royal Society of Literature in 2000. Her illustrated autobiography, *A Life Drawing*, was published in 2002.

Eva Ibbotson (b. 1925) was born in Vienna and came with her family to Britain before the Second World War. A writer of short stories and adult historical fiction as well as children's books, her much praised children's novel *Journey to the River Sea* was awarded the Nestlé Smarties Gold Award in 2001.

Dick King-Smith (b. 1922) began writing late in life – he was previously a soldier, a primary school teacher and a farmer. A prolific writer of over fifty books, he is widely known for his witty animal stories – and perhaps best known of all for *The Sheep-Pig*, which won the Guardian Children's Fiction Award in 1984.

Satoshi Kitamura (b. 1956) was born in Tokyo and has worked in Britain since 1979. All his picture books have been published in the UK first and then in Japan, translated by Satoshi from English into Japanese. He has received many awards, including the Mother Goose Award for *Angry Arthur* in 1982.

Wes Magee (b. 1939) is a former primary school teacher, anthologist and poet and spends much time visiting schools. He is also author of the inventive and amusing *Scumbagg School* stories. His latest poetry collection for children is *The Phantom's Fang-tastic Show*. He reviews regularly for *Carousel*.

Jan Mark (b. 1943) was awarded the Carnegie Medal with her first book for children, *Thunder and Lightnings*, and has won many other prizes since then. Her work never underestimates the reader or patronizes them and is for those who like stories with a bite – either a comic twist or a tragic one. She also finds time to review regularly for *Carousel*.

Geraldine McCaughrean (b.1951) began work in publishing and later turned to writing for both adults and children on a full-time basis. *Stop the Train* is, for the present, her favourite novel. She has won many prizes including the inaugural Blue Peter Book of the Year Award for her retelling of *Pilgrim's Progress*.

Judith Nicholls (b.1941) was a teacher before she made her debut as a writer with *Magic Mirror* in 1985. She is now well known as an anthologist and poet and has written more than fifty books. She also enjoys reviewing for *Carousel*.

Jack Ousbey (b. 1930) is a teacher, lecturer, adviser, inspector;

contributor to educational readers and university journals; consultant to Anne Wood's Ragdoll U.K. company; reviewer for *Carousel* and part-time rhymer.

Helen Oxenbury (b. 1938) is a picture book author and illustrator often closely associated with books for pre-school children. She has won many awards including the Kurt Maschler Award in 1999 and the Kate Greenaway Medal in 2000 for her modern interpretation of *Alice in Wonderland*.

Korky Paul (b. 1951) grew up scribbling in Zimbabwe and studied Fine Art and Film Animation. He has illustrated the *Winnie the Witch* books by Valerie Thomas, winner of the Children's Book Award, and others for Oxford, Penguin and Random House, including anthologies of poetry. He is useless as a writer and is known (only to himself) as the world's greatest portrait artist. www.korkypaul.com

Chris Powling (b. 1943) is a children's author, broadcaster and critic. He is equally at home writing for teenagers and early readers. One of his most popular books is *The Phantom Carwash*; he has also written the biography of Roald Dahl. Chris contributes regularly to *Carousel*.

Chris Riddell (b. 1962) studied under Raymond Briggs at Brighton Polytechnic and has developed a dual career as an illustrator and political cartoonist for the *Observer*. He collaborates with Paul Stewart on the *Edge Chronicles*. He was awarded the 2001 Kate Greenaway Medal for *Pirate Diary*, the first time an information book has won the award for twenty-seven years.

Tony Ross (b. 1938) is a prolific illustrator of both his own stories and those of other authors. He is the illustrator for Jeanne Willis's *Dr Xargle* series; produced a series of retold and updated fairy tales and been awarded many prizes including the Dutch Silver Pencil Award for *I Want My Potty* in 1987. Many of his books have been read and partially animated for television.

Nick Sharratt (b. 1962) is the distinctive illustrator of both Jacqueline Wilson's and Jeremy Strong's books. He has produced many picture books in his own right, some of which experiment with split pages or cut-outs. He was awarded the 2001 Children's Book Award for *Eat Your Peas* by Kes Gray.

Jeremy Strong (b. 1949) is an ex-head teacher who produces stories of great humour with catastrophic chaos on one side and the issues of bullying, low self-esteem or family loyalty on the other. He was the Children's Book Award winner in 1997 with *The Hundred-Mile-an-Hour Dog*. www.jeremystrong.co.uk

Robert Swindells (b. 1939) was born in Yorkshire and wrote his first book in 1973. Many of his stories are characterized by unease about contemporary society. He has won the Children's Book Award twice and in 1993 received the Carnegie Medal for *Stone Cold*, the research for which involved living rough in London for a week.

Nick Toczek (b. 1950) has been a writer and performer for the past thirty-five years. During that time he has published more than two dozen books – most recently *Kick It!*, a collection of his football poems. He has made almost 30,000 public appearances and has visited thousands of schools. He is also a magician and puppeteer, and occasionally reviews for *Carousel*.

Kaye Umansky (b. 1946) has been a drama teacher, a television presenter for educational programmes and singer in a band as well as writing for children. She has written plays, musicals, books of songs and novels – *Pongwiffy, a Witch with Dirty Habits* is one of her most popular books.

Jacqueline Wilson (b. 1945) is an influential and popular children's author. Winning the Children's Book Award in 1993 with *The Suitcase Kid* was a milestone in her career and she has since garnered many awards. She deals with difficult situations in which children may find themselves, written with humour and from a child's perspective.